I0760786

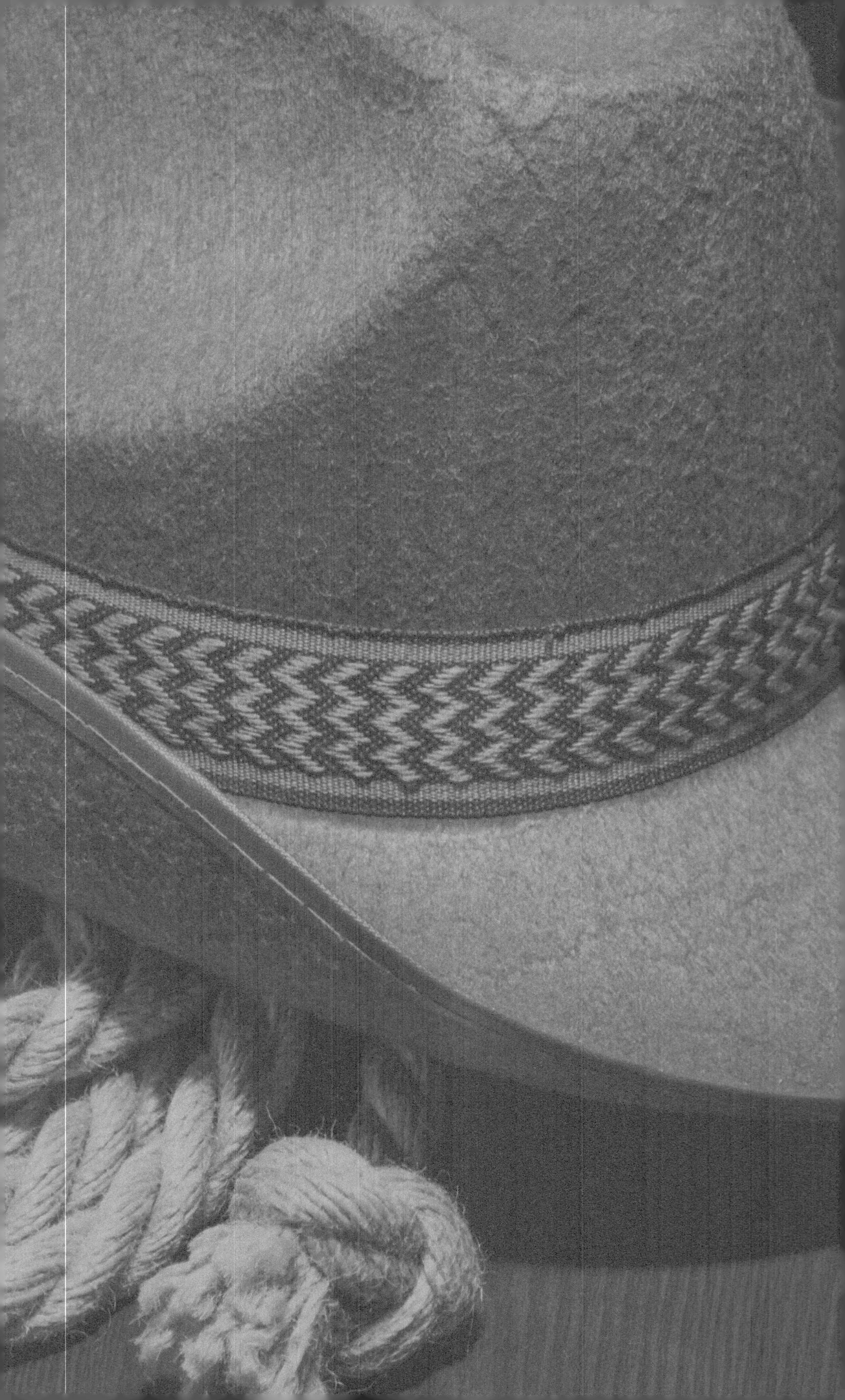

Twisted Cross Ranch Book Three

Deadly Debt

K. Loraine

USA Today bestselling authors

Meg Anne

This book is a work of fiction. The names, characters, places, and incidents are products of the author's imagination or have been used fictitiously and are not to be construed as real. Any resemblance to persons, living or dead, actual events, locales, or organizations is entirely coincidental.

Alternate Cover Edition.

ISBN:

978-1-961742-10-9 (Paperback Edition)

978-1-961742-11-6 (Hardback Edition)

Edited by Mo Sytsma of Comma Sutra Editorial

Cover Design by T.E. Black Designs

To the FBI. Don't @ us about our search history. It was for the book, you can check our receipts
(except for that one tab, give that one a pass).
Also, sorry for the creative license. Your rules are complicated and not conducive to happy endings. And dammit, they earned one.

"I believe in lovin' with your whole soul and destroying anything that wants to kill what you love. That's it. That's all there is."

— Beth Dutton, Yellowstone

deadly debt

K. LORAINE
USA TODAY BESTSELLING AUTHORS
MEG ANNE

authors' note

Pssst…over here darlin'. We know you're eager to dive in (especially after the way we left that last one) but we wanted to get a little housekeeping out of the way first.

As always please be advised that Deadly Debt contains mature and graphic content that may not be suitable for all readers. Such content includes kidnapping, human trafficking, attempted SA, group sex, PTSD, murder, and more. A detailed list of content and trigger warnings is available on our website.

And second, for the sake of fiction and compelling storytelling, we've taken some liberties with regards to the inner workings of these government agencies and their procedures. Just like not all firefighters are hot, not all FBI agents bend the rules to ensure an HEA. But we know what you crave, darlin', and we want to give you the ending you deserve. Procedures and protocol be damned. We're all here for an escape, right? Reality can suck it.

Okay, now that that's out of the way, back to the reason we're all here:

Hot, dirty cowboys. We hope you enjoy the thrilling conclusion of Twisted Cross Ranch as much as we enjoyed writing it.

K & M

one

• • •

Bishop

The dank, dingy hall was cold and smelled of wet earth and mildew as I crept noiselessly toward my target. My flashlight's beam revealed nothing but cement and a single door as far as the eye could see. Eventually I'd reach her. All my intel said she was being kept here.

I just hoped I wasn't too late.

The steel door at the far end was calling me. I could practically hear her voice beckoning me. Begging me.

I'm coming.

I'm here.

Just hang on.

Sweat dripped down the back of my neck as I moved as quickly as I could, my trigger finger tense and ready in case any of those assholes tried to get the jump on me. All signs pointed to them having bolted, which was another frustration for the team. We'd been made before we could bring the fuckers in, but at least we'd found her.

Reaching the door, I bit the end of my flashlight so I could keep the light trained down but also freeing my hand so I could grab and pull the bar locking it. For a heavy slab of metal, it slid open soundlessly.

The smell hit me first.

Sweat, blood, piss, and . . . cum.

I shuddered as revulsion rolled through me, followed quickly by fury. They'd hurt her in every way possible. When I found them, I wouldn't bring them to justice. I'd make them pay. Slowly. Agonizingly. Terribly.

Taking the flashlight in hand once more, I swept the beam across the small cell, stopping on the curled-up female form on a dirty mattress in the corner.

My heart lurched at the sight of her.

She was barely covered by a T-shirt. What I could see of her emaciated limbs was a riot of bruises, all in various stages of healing. Her hair was so dirty it was impossible to tell what color it was.

Fuck.

Holstering my gun, I rushed forward, my usual greeting on the tip of my tongue.

Ma'am, I'm Special Agent Sterling Bishop. I'm here to rescue you.

But the words turned to ash in my mouth.

She was still.

Too still.

The underlying scent of death, mixed with the rest of the odors in this prison, came to the forefront now that I was closer.

"No. Fuck. Please. Don't let me be too late."

With a gentle hand, I touched her icy shoulder as I rolled her onto her back. Purple bruises marred the graceful column of her throat, her skin a lifeless gray, mottled on one side where the blood had settled.

And her eyes. Those beautiful green eyes I'd fallen in love with were a lifeless, clouded white.

"River!"

Her name was a scream and a denial as I shot up in bed, sweat soaking through my tank and the tangled sheets beneath me. My heart pounded so hard my chest hurt, and my pulse roared in my ears.

It wasn't River. It couldn't have been. The nightmare was one I'd had often, especially in the months following that failed rescue attempt years ago. My failure haunted me, the woman's cold body locked in my memory like a ghost. Her name had been Joy Franklin. Age twenty-two. Just starting her life as an up-and-coming artist. Until her boyfriend sold her to the Russian mob to pay off his gambling debts.

She wasn't the only person I'd ever lost, but she'd been the first. It didn't take a shrink to figure out that losing River to the same bastards had triggered my PTSD from that mission. Only this time, my subconscious was replacing Joy's face with hers. Warning me of what the outcome would be if I failed again.

My hands fisted in the sheets.

I *could not* fail.

Not this time.

My siren had been gone seven days. That meant she'd endured a week of torture at their hands. I was all too familiar with what they could do to the human body and how little they cared about their captives.

There was no line they wouldn't cross. Drugs. Beatings. Rape.

These women were nothing but a means to an end.

Every second that ticked by weighed on me. It was another second closer to finding her curled up on that mattress. Beyond help.

Nerves shot, I knew I wouldn't be able to get any more sleep tonight. The clock on my dresser read three a.m., which was only a few hours before I normally woke anyway. If I couldn't rescue River right this minute, I could at least keep myself fit and ready for a fight. A punishing run on the treadmill and a weightlifting session would keep my mind sharp and focused.

Even though I was just going to sweat through them again, I changed out of my clothes into a fresh pair of gym shorts and a T-shirt before slipping on a pair of sneakers.

Conscious of the time, I made sure my steps were silent as I wandered down the hall on my way to the gym. I shouldn't have worried, though, because the light in the formal living room was on, and the Cross brothers' voices floated out to me.

Guess I wasn't the only one not sleeping much these days.

Instead of continuing to the gym, I stopped when I heard my name, turning toward the two men. They looked fucking broken. Just as broken as me. Walker's hair was a wild tangle, his jaw covered in heavy stubble, expression drawn as he placed his rocks glass on the coffee table in front of him. Cross appeared no better. The man was usually more together than anyone I'd known, crisp and clean, buttoned up and polished. Now? He looked like he'd gone six rounds with an angry bull and lost.

Cross was dressed for business, but the way his sleeves were rolled up to his elbows and the number of wrinkles marring his western shirt betrayed just how long he'd been wearing these clothes. Had the man even slept? The empty decanter on the table in front of him would suggest not.

He didn't seem drunk, though. More like he was just trying to keep his emotions in check while everything was spiraling out of control.

I was about to let them know I was there when Walker kept talking. They hadn't seen me; they'd been talking about me. And they were pissed.

"Are you sure we should trust him? He said we have a mole. What if it's him?"

"I don't fucking know. He cares about her. You've seen it yourself. Why would he let them take her?" Cross dropped his head into his hands and heaved a sigh. "It doesn't track. And he saved your ass twice."

"He's a fucking spy, Cross."

"I fucking know, Walker."

"He checked out on paper. Shit. I thought a former SEAL would be good to have in our corner. Hell, he didn't even use a fake name. How were we supposed to know he was a fed?"

I stiffened, wondering where they'd gotten their intel. Not that it really mattered. As for my name, Wilson had offered me a cover, but I'd declined it. After my time as his prisoner, there was no way Volkov would forget my face. A new name wasn't gonna do a damn thing to hide me. Wilson ultimately agreed, and if anything, showing up at Twisted Cross Ranch as myself lended my story credibility.

"It doesn't matter. What's done is done. But River's fallen for him, and he'll turn us in before we get her back if we show our hand. What do you want me to do? Kick him out?"

"It's not the worst idea. I mean, he's been hiding in plain sight. A fucking fox in our hen house, making fools of us all. We can't trust him."

"With his connections and training, he's one of the few people who might be able to track down the fucker who took our woman."

"So he says. What good is that fancy title of his? He's found out fuck all so far. Volkov is in the wind. We haven't heard so much as a damn peep from the Russians. We may as well be sitting here with our thumbs up our asses. It's been a week. Where is she? People don't just up and vanish, dammit."

Cross let out a grumble before reaching for the decanter, stopping himself, and sighing. "I've never been this fucking lost. My instincts are screaming at me to set the world on fire, but I'm afraid any act of retaliation on my part will only get her killed. I don't know what to do."

My phone vibrated in my pocket, taking me back into the hall so I was hidden in the shadows. I was in enemy territory right now; best to play it smart. They knew more than I'd suspected, but I wasn't surprised they'd dug up the truth. I'd all but admitted it myself the night she'd been taken.

Glancing at the screen, my pulse picked up at the text I'd received.

WILSON:

We have a hit on the package. Call me.

two

. . .

Cross

My eyes burned as I stared at the silent phone on the coffee table, willing it to ring. Desperate for some kind of word that River had been found or even a ransom note from fucking Volkov. I just needed something that would put a stop to the endless waiting. I hated being helpless. It was weak, and I was anything but weak.

Walker and I had been sitting in utter silence for the last hour after our conversation. We'd gone round and round and basically ended up back where we started. In this weird fucking limbo where nothing mattered but finding her. Neither of us wanted to sleep in case she miraculously showed up at the house. We wouldn't entertain getting her back any way but whole.

The fire had died down due to our inattention, but I couldn't find it in myself to get up and put another log on. Instead, I watched the flames dance, their soft crackle a soothing lull despite the unpredictable pops of sap. I must have been more out of it than I thought because I hadn't heard the footsteps until Bishop's towering frame was right beside us.

"What the hell do you want?" I snarled, my anger with myself compounding the mistrust I had toward him, especially after McCreedy's phone call a few days earlier.

Bishop wasn't just former military. He was a fed and he was here to take us down.

"I've got a lead."

"Your secret agent buddies help you with that?" Walker asked, eyes narrowed. "How do we know you didn't take her and hide her away so we would walk right into your trap?"

He raised a single, unimpressed brow. "If I wanted to haul your asses in, I'd do it right now. No trap required. You two have more blood on your hands than half the fucking state."

"Why don't you then?"

"Because whether you believe me or not, all I care about is finding River. Arresting the two of you doesn't get me any closer to that end."

"Your friends at the FBI must love you playing both sides like that."

"Maybe, if they knew about it."

"So we're just supposed to take your word for it? Believe you're not going to turn around and screw us? Why are you even still here, Bishop?"

I couldn't disagree with my brother. But the truth was, Bishop had been here, a wolf in sheep's clothing, for months now. Gathering intel, fucking helping me with our shipments, and learning all about our dirty deeds. He knew who we were involved with, how deep we were in, and whether we got River back or not, he could send us to prison for a long fucking time.

"Just give us until River is safe," I said, my voice calm and cold. "That's all we need. Then you can turn us in and get your goddamn gold star for being a good boy."

Walker stared at me in shock. "You're just going to roll over and show your belly? You're not even going to fight for her?" He shook his head in disgust. "You don't fucking deserve her, man."

He was right. I didn't. And after this, there was no way she would want to be with me anyway. I was the reason she was in this mess. She was better off without me. But he was missing the point. We had nothing if we lost her.

"I'd rather she be safe and with him than dead or in Volkov's hands, Walk. Bishop has probably already delivered enough intel on us to send us away for a long time."

Bishop cleared his throat. "I haven't, actually."

"What?"

"Sent anything incriminating in."

"Why the fuck not?" Walker asked, glancing at me. "Don't get me wrong, I'm relieved to hear it, but . . . isn't that sort of what you do?"

"Everything I've seen since I've been here points to the two of you not being as involved as originally suspected. So my evidence doesn't actually help their case."

That was bullshit, but I wasn't going to argue. "So you're really going to help us get her back?"

He nodded. "I'm in. All fucking in. They took my woman, and I'm going to make them pay. What the feds don't know won't hurt them, but it sure as shit will feel good when I put a bullet through Volkov's skull."

I raised a brow, needing to be sure he knew what he was getting himself into. "You're really ready to blow your entire life up? Just like that?"

"She *is* my life."

Fair enough. She was mine too. Even if I would have to spend the rest of it without her.

"I still don't trust you as far as I can throw you." Walker stood, the cane he was using to support him the only thing keeping him on his feet. He wasn't ready for this, but the man wouldn't be told otherwise.

"You'll have to if we're gonna get her back."

"You gotta plan?" I asked.

Bishop waved his phone at us. "Like I said. I've got a lead. We got a hit on Volkov."

"You know where he is?" I said, voice deadly soft as I got to my feet, suddenly on high alert.

"Maybe."

"Where?"

"A remote location outside El Paso."

"What are we waiting for? Let's go get her," Walker said, taking an unsteady step toward the front door.

"I've already got guys on it, investigating the lead, but it's better than nothing."

I was itching to go after her too, just like my brother. Nothing was worse than this feeling of being caged.

"So what the fuck are we supposed to do in the meantime?" Walker asked, frustration evident in the tightness of his voice.

"It's too risky to go ourselves," Bishop said, sounding just as put out. "Trust me, I want to go too. But we can't show our hand yet. He catches word we're onto him, it could spook him, and then our leads will dry up again. It's better this way."

As much as I hated it, he was right. My stomach was a pit of cold fear at the thought of losing any thread of connection to her location.

"You'd better tell us everything you find out as soon as you hear. I'm not interested in waiting around for you to decide we need to know."

He nodded. "You have my word."

"For what that's worth," Walker muttered, maneuvering himself back to the couch where he gracelessly plopped down.

Bishop's expression didn't change, but I caught the slight tensing of his shoulders before he gave me a little nod and left me and my brother alone.

"We're fucked. You know that, right?" Walker asked, head in his hands.

"We were the moment she set foot on our property."

My brother heaved a sigh and reached into his pocket, pulling out a black velvet pouch before shoving it at me. "Here. You should have this."

A frown tugged at my lips as I opened the little bag and dumped the contents into my palm. "Is this Mama's ring?" I asked, head snapping up so I could look at him.

His eyes were locked on the pretty piece of jewelry cradled in my hand. "Yup."

"You went into her room? I haven't been in there since she died." I trailed my fingers over the sparkling diamond, my heart in my throat. She'd been everything to us. Dad hadn't been the same after she died. None of us had.

"River deserves to wear that ring. I was gonna give it to her." Walker shrugged. "Now you get to. If she's married to a Cross, she should have the ring meant for a Cross woman."

Mouth suddenly dry, I couldn't answer him. The image of River wearing this ring had my heart thumping erratically. It would be perfect for her. It was as rare and special as she was. But even as hope ignited at the thought she might wear it one day, it died out just as fast.

She wouldn't want it if it came from me.

I didn't fucking deserve to give it to her.

"You keep it. She was forced to marry me. She can choose to marry you."

Walker's brows dropped low over confused eyes. "She can't be married to both of us. This is still Texas, you know."

I knew all too well. "Leave that to me."

Walker missed my meaning with a soft chuckle. "Your name carries weight, but I don't think you can get a whole-ass law changed. Polygamy is still sort of taboo in these parts." Then his smile faltered, and he shook his head. "Do you ever wonder why Senior did it? Married the two of you in secret like that?"

"Every damn day. But honestly, I'm afraid of the answer. I sort of chalked it up to his going off the deep end after Mama died and left it at that."

"Yeah," Walker breathed. "You never did tell me what happened that night. After the party."

Ice running through my veins, I swallowed. "I kept you in the dark for a reason. You were too young for the shit I saw. It was bad, Walk. So fucking bad that I made sure River never wanted to come back here. Dad messed everything up for us. He dug us into a hole so deep with the Russians, I'm not sure we can ever get ourselves out."

A strange expression crossed my brother's face. "So that's what they were talking about."

three

. . .

Walker

Ten years earlier

I snagged a glass of champagne off a nearby server's tray, wincing as I gulped it down, eyes locked on the pretty blonde who'd stolen my heart. River stood near the patio doors, all smiles as she celebrated her birthday. Her mama adjusted the skirt of River's dress, then cupped her cheek, smiling with unmistakable pride as she pulled my ladybug in for an embrace. I'd be lying if I said a lick of jealousy didn't go through me at the sight. I missed my mama. So damn much.

Elsie was one of the kindest souls I'd ever known, and watching the two of them together right now, it was clear where River got her heart. Elsie murmured something in River's ear, and she nodded before breaking away and heading toward Dad's office. I couldn't help but watch her go. And apparently, neither could my brother.

Cross was leaning against the banister at the base of the stairs, half-listening to Jackson with a full bottle of whiskey in his hand. He stared after her with a strange intensity in his eyes I'd never noticed before.

I'd seen that hunger often enough in hers, usually when she was lusting after him. But never the other way around. Until tonight. When she was legally old enough for him to ruin her.

Fuck.

Tonight had not gone to plan. Not at all.

I was supposed to be balls deep in Daisy Stewart, fucking my way out of love with my best friend. Instead, I caught one look at River in that white party dress, and my dick forgot how to function for anyone else. Truth be told, that had been the case since I realized I was head over heels for her.

Goddammit. All I wanted was to move on from this tortured heart character I felt like I'd been typecast as. Whoever was writing my storyline really needed to give me a damn break. Weren't you supposed to be the main character in your own life? So why was I stuck playing second fiddle to my older brother?

Because everyone knows Cross is the better one. He's smarter, more shrewd, better looking. You're the one they throw away.

My inner voice knew just where to land the blows.

Leaving the empty glass on the first available surface, I took a fortifying breath. If I couldn't fall for another girl, maybe I could distract myself with other things. Like diving headfirst into the family business rather than what I had been doing, dipping my toe in here and there. I could prove my worth to Senior. Make him see I was just as useful as Cross, show him he could be proud I had his name.

Because all your prior attempts were so successful.

I groaned, wishing I could beat the shit out of my inner saboteur. Sometimes those intrusive thoughts got so loud I forgot they weren't real. That it was my insecurity and a lifetime of feeling like I was destined to be second-best coming back to haunt me.

Maybe tonight would be a good night to try and clear the air with my dad. Let him know I was ready for more responsibility. That I was all in, more than just a Cross boy in name. Perhaps he'd just been waiting for me to take a little initiative all this time. Sounded like something he'd do. Set me up to disappoint him.

Not this time.

Daisy sidled up next to me, offering a fresh drink and a sweet smile as she did. I barely noticed her, going through the motions as she talked at me. I nodded at the right times, made agreeable noises, drank, and smiled. But I wasn't really present in the moment.

The cacophony of this party swirled around me—chatter, music, laughter, the clink of glasses, and, of course, River's presence. She owned so much of me it was ridiculous.

Speaking of, I noticed her the second she returned to the party. She was beelining her way through the foyer, stopping only long enough to grab a glass of champagne from the same server as I had. She finished it quickly, then glanced around, her eyes never straying far enough to spot me, before she made her escape out the front. I couldn't tell if she was searching for someone or hiding from them. I'd have to go ask her just as soon as I talked to my father.

"Excuse me, darlin'," I said, interrupting Daisy mid-sentence.

I didn't bother waiting for a reply. It wasn't like I was interested in anything she had to say to me anyway. That train left the station the second I came to terms with the fact my heart would always belong to another woman. And Daisy deserved better than a guy who was pining for someone else.

I strode down the hall toward my father's office, knowing he'd be holding court there. He was rarely anywhere else during these sorts of events. They were usually just excuses to lubricate potential business partners before making them an offer they couldn't refuse. Senior didn't have much of a stomach for social events after my mother died. From what Cross had told me, she was the one who shined in those situations; everyone else had been drawn into her orbit. My father included.

Raising my hand to knock, I stopped at the sound of voices coming from the cracked door. Casey and Dad were deep in conversation, and I almost turned around until I heard River's name.

"She won't understand when she finds out," Casey said.

"Her safety is worth her anger, don't you think?"

"And Cross?"

"He understands it's a business arrangement. He's on board."

"You told him?"

"Not in so many words, but he's a good boy, and he trusts me. He'll do what he's told."

I couldn't quite see them, but Casey's sigh was long and heavy. "I just hope we're doing the right thing."

"A merger like this sets her up for life. She won't ever want for anything. Besides . . . you know what's on the line."

"You're right." Another drawn-out sigh. "This is the only way to protect my family."

"Debts are a deadly business, Casey. A man must always ensure his ledger is clear."

There was a rustling sound, like papers moving around. "Thank you, D. I'll never be able to repay you." Something about the tone of Casey's voice made me think this was far more than a simple business transaction.

"You already did. No need to speak of it ever again. Just make sure this gets to Volkov, and maybe next time you get the urge to play poker, we fly to Vegas instead."

Casey laughed, but it was a hollow sound. "I think my gambling days are over."

"Even better. Now let's get out there and enjoy your daughter's party. I've got a couple of cigars with our names on them."

Adrenaline spiked in my veins. I shouldn't have fucking been there. I'd heard way more than enough to know that. Before the two of them caught me eavesdropping, I turned on my heel and walked away as fast as I could.

I'd talk to my father later.

Tomorrow, maybe.

Yeah, tomorrow was good.

Present day

THE MEMORY FADED, leaving me speechless on the couch beside my brother. "It makes so much sense now," I murmured.

"What does?" Cross asked, expression stormy, voice hollow.

"It wasn't Dad. It was Casey."

That seemed to get his attention. Cross blinked, his gaze sharpening on me. "Explain."

"Casey was in trouble with the Russians. Gambling debt, I think. I don't have all the details, but if I had to bet, Dad helped him pay it off."

"How do you fucking know that?"

"I overheard them the night of the party. It was buried so far in my memories I'd forgotten until you mentioned it. Casey was talking about keeping her safe and thanking Dad for helping him. I thought they were talking about a business merger, but I think . . . Jesus, I think they were talking about your marriage. If Volkov wanted to get his hands on River, maybe as payment for Casey's debt, then this is way more personal than we thought. If they have her, Cross, there's no telling what they're gonna do."

Chills erupted across my body, a cold, clammy sweat starting at the base of my spine and creeping along my skin. Panic followed, clutching my lungs and making it hard to breathe. I didn't want to remember what they did to me, but knowing Volkov likely had River, I couldn't keep those thoughts from intruding. Then another detail swam up, pulling me back to the present.

"Wait, but that was ten years ago. Luca was still running things back then. Why would he care about River at all? There was no reason for her to even be on his radar."

Cross's expression was grave as his eyes bore into mine. "There was only one thing Luca cared about more than his money, and that was his nephew. He was his heir, after all."

It all clicked into place, and my stomach rolled. "The sonofabitch wanted her for him."

Cross nodded. "Which is why Dom's got his sights set on her now. Fucker's probably convinced she belongs to him. Fuck!" he shouted, banging his hand down on the coffee table and making the empty glasses rattle from the force. "That's what that asshole meant when he asked if I was sure she was mine."

"We have to find her, Cross. The things they did . . ." I couldn't get the rest out. He'd seen the truth with his own eyes when those assholes dumped me at the gate. Every inch of the destruction they'd done to my body. No one but him and the doctor knew how close I'd been to dying. And maybe Bishop. He knew a lot more about what had happened to me than anyone else, seeing as how he'd suffered the same.

"I'm not fucking resting until she's back here where she belongs. She's ours, Walker. No one steals from us and gets away with it."

It was the first time since she'd been taken he'd referred to her as ours, and I believed him. Piece by piece, I'd been watching him fall into himself, likely trying to convince himself to play the martyr. To let her go, give her an out because he felt guilty he'd gotten her into this.

But now he knew that it wasn't his fault at all. It was her father's.

And that gave him an excuse to fight.

Good. I needed my brother all in. I needed the man that made grown men piss themselves in fear when he walked into a room.

I had a feeling it was the only way we'd ever get her back.

four

• • •

River

"That's right, sparrow. Open up for us. I've been dying to stretch you out again." Cross's voice rolled through my mind, drugging me with its seductive rasp.

Walker's grip on my hips tightened. "Wait your turn. Can't you see she's busy?"

"I thought the point of this arrangement was that no one has to wait," Bishop said, his fingers gliding down my spine. The touch sent tingles racing over my skin, making my nipples harden on reflex. "Fuck, look at that. So responsive. They look like ripe berries, perfect and delicious."

"Why don't you take a taste?" I teased, but my words were breathy and stilted as Walker lifted me up and notched his swollen cock at my entrance.

Bishop did, the wet heat of his mouth a perfect contrast to the rough scratch of Cross's stubbled jaw as he nipped the side of my neck.

"So wet for us, darlin'. You ready to go for a ride?"

Walker didn't even wait for me to answer, sliding inside me in one smooth thrust, his piercing lighting me up as it rubbed against all the best spots.

"Oh, God."

My moans were swallowed by Bishop's kiss, his hands now tangled in my hair as his tongue danced with mine. Walker's cock jerked inside me, hips rutting upward in search of a way to get even deeper inside. God, I wanted this. I wanted *them*.

Cross's lips trailed over my shoulder blade, then down my spine, until he kissed each of the dimples just over the swell of my ass, his fingers running across my lower belly until he found my clit.

"Lean forward, sweetness. I need to see all of you."

Bishop released me, helping me lay down on top of Walker, who eagerly wrapped me in his arms, his lips feasting on mine. Sterling continued to stroke my hair, offering silent encouragement while Walker lazily thrust in and out of me.

"Christ," Cross grunted, his fingers dipping between my ass cheeks, pausing to press against my virgin hole. "Has anyone had you here before?"

"N-no. I . . . no one's touched me like that."

I could feel the smirk before he let out a dark chuckle. "Such a good girl, saving all your firsts for me."

"Not all," Bishop corrected. "I'm the one who taught her how to suck a dick."

"Thanks for that," Walker said, his voice strained. "She's a fucking champ."

"Yeah, she is," Cross agreed.

Walker did something with his hips, and I wailed as pleasure ricocheted through me.

"Fuck, Cross, stop teasing her. She's so tight. She's gonna make me come before this really gets started."

"I'm not teasing her. I'm warming her up. If she's going to take both of us at once, we need to make sure she can handle it."

And then, his mouth was *there*, tongue tracing the rim of my hole, making me gasp at the forbidden sensation. He pulled away before I was ready, but he didn't move far, spreading my cheeks wider apart.

"What are you doing?" I panted.

"Can't you tell, siren? He's spitting on you. Needs to lube you up before he works his fingers inside you."

"Oh, God." I rolled my eyes up to meet Bishop's. The look of pure lust on his face had me clenching around Walker as Cross's warm saliva trailed down my crack.

Walker whimpered, then grunted, "Jesus fucking Christ, darlin'. You're killing me."

"If you blow, I'll just take your place," Bishop offered.

The thought of that was enough to have my walls clenching again.

"Shh, relax, baby," Cross said, the blunt tip of one finger pressing into me.

I moaned. It was all I could do as he worked it inside slowly.

"It's too much," I protested.

"You know how big I am. If you want us both, I have to stretch you."

I nodded, too incoherent to form words when he added a second finger.

"Don't move a fucking muscle, ladybug. I swear to God, I'm holding on for dear life here. You squeeze me so good. Are you trying to milk my cock?"

It was all so much. The filthy words, their hands on me, all at the same time. Even still, I wanted more. I wanted everything.

"Please," I gasped, not entirely sure what I was asking for, but trusting them to know.

Bishop ran a thumb over my jaw, stopping when he reached my lips. He slipped the digit between them, eyes hot as he stared at me. "You look so pretty stuffed full, but you'd be even prettier with my dick in your throat."

"Yes," I agreed, desperate to have them all inside me.

Still holding my gaze, he gave himself a few lazy strokes before rubbing the crown of his cock along my bottom lip. A bead of precum spread over my mouth, and I couldn't resist; I flicked my tongue out to taste him. Salty and potent. Exactly like I remembered.

"Open wide, sugar. I've got a present for you."

As I took him into my mouth, a stream of liquid spilled over my ass. Lube, I realized. Thank God.

Bishop groaned when I let out a hum of surprise as Cross's dick slid between my cheeks. And then I was the one groaning as he forced his thick length inside.

Walker let out a stream of unintelligible curses, which I echoed in my soul. I knew exactly what he meant. The added pressure, the intensity of the dueling glides in and out of me as they found their rhythm. It was nirvana. I was going to die of pleasure.

"Fuck, I love you, River," Cross grunted. "You take us so fucking good. You were made for us."

"Me too. I love you so much, darlin'. I wanna live here and never leave," Walker said through gritted teeth.

"Never gonna let you go. You're ours. Forever." Bishop's cock swelled in my mouth as Cross gripped my hips hard enough it hurt.

"We're gonna fill you so full of our cum it'll be dripping out of you for days," Cross growled.

I moaned my approval, silently begging them to do just that. I was so close to my own climax, but I wanted all of us to go off together.

Agony burst across my side, bright and sharp. "Wake the fuck up, bitch."

My eyes flew open, the refuge of my fantasy instantly taken over by the nightmare of my reality. Gone were the cozy loft and my three protective lovers. In their place was a dank and dingy cell that smelled of mildew and despair.

No. I don't want to be here. Let me go back. I want to be with them.

I already knew better than to give voice to my prayers. All they did was bring me more pain.

My kidnapper, Pytor, hovered over me, his face twisted in its usual scowl. "Eat." He shoved a water bottle and plate at me. Both fell in my lap, my limbs sluggish from the effects of sleep and sedatives. Not that I had much of an appetite for the moldy ham and cheese sandwich he'd brought me anyway.

I'd lost track of the days; everything blurred together here. But I supposed that made sense since there were no windows to tell me what time of day it was. He kept me drugged for the most part, feeding me once a day, if I was lucky, and coming to empty my . . . bucket.

"Wh-why are you doing this?" I managed to get out through my dry throat.

He sneered, disgust on his face. "He told me to. Now shut up and eat. You need your strength."

"For what?"

But he didn't answer me. I didn't expect him to; he rarely did.

Instead he stormed back out, slamming and locking the door behind him.

Staring at the meager offering he'd brought me, I shoved it away. The drugs were in the water, that much I'd figured out. But if I didn't drink it, I'd die of dehydration, or they'd simply shoot me up with a needle. I'd woken up once attached to an IV with fluids running directly to my vein. They wanted me alive, that much was certain, and I couldn't outsmart them. Nor could I win in a fight.

I'd stopped crying after what I thought was the second day, my tears burning away in light of my rage. But then I lost that too. Now I was merely surviving. Trying to stay alert long enough to plan an escape or outwit my kidnappers, but ultimately succumbing to the drugs. At least in my dreams, I could see my men again. Could say all the things I'd never had a chance to say in person.

At least when I was sleeping, I was free.

Numb and hollow, I reached for the water, twisting open the cap before I drained half the bottle in one long swallow. Then I curled up into a ball once more, praying I'd find them again in my dreams.

Somewhere out there, I knew they were looking for me. That they wouldn't stop until they found me. I just hoped there'd be something left of me to find.

five

• • •

Cross

I handed off Hades's reins to Tommy after finishing my ride, giving him a curt nod and a grunt for his efforts. I'd hoped to distract myself from the hell I was living in by getting outside, breathing fresh air, and centering myself on the back of my horse. It didn't fucking work. I was still the angry, bitter, frustrated man I'd always been.

Okay, that's not strictly true; I was way fucking worse. But recent circumstances hadn't exactly been easy. First my father's unexpected death, then River's reappearance in my life, then the marriage bombshell, Walker's attacks—plural—all of Volkov's bullshit, culminating in her kidnapping. I was one secret twin away from starring in my own soap opera. Jesus, knowing Dad, I just might have a secret sibling out there somewhere. Or he'd pop back into our lives six months down the road to tell us this was all some sort of fucked up test and he wasn't really dead. Goddammit. My chest was so tight I could barely breathe.

My phone rang almost as soon as I stepped into the house, McCreedy's name flashing on the screen.

"What?" I barked.

"You need to do something about the hellion who just stormed into my office."

"Excuse me? Since when is anything that happens at your office my fucking problem?"

"Since your *wife* is the reason this particular problem made an appearance."

I squeezed the bridge of my nose and released a strained breath. "I have no idea what you're talking about."

"Allow me to enlighten you. Ever hear of one Virginia Blake?"

"My name is Gigi, asshole."

"Excuse me, Gigi Blake, sister of one Jonah Blake."

"Bear!" she growled, though it came through loud and clear, as if she was standing at his shoulder shouting into the phone right alongside him.

Shit. No one told her. Bear's sister was here, and she didn't know he'd been killed.

My day just went from natural disaster to apocalypse on the shit trying to take me out scale.

"Jackson, you need to keep her occupied."

"What? No way. I'm due in court in an hour. I can't babysit her."

"Bullshit. It's already after five."

"She's been here hours already, wouldn't budge from the lobby. My assistant had to threaten to call the cops, and even then, this demon wasn't put off. You wouldn't know it to look at her, but she's got a temper that would rival your own."

"I'll show you a fucking temper, you trumped-up snake oil salesman." Gigi's voice was venom laced and held no hint of a bluff.

On any other day, it would have made me smile. She clearly took after her brother. I was starting to piece together how she and River became such fast friends. But it wasn't any other day, and this was one problem I did not have time to deal with.

"Sounds like you've got yourself a shadow for the foreseeable future. Sorry to say, my dance card is full."

"Where the fuck is River?" she shouted, clearly meaning the question for me.

"Tell her River's not here. Neither is her brother."

"When are they getting back?" she asked, not needing McCreedy to pass along the message. He must have put me on speaker, the coward.

A vein pulsed in my neck, and I had to fight to keep my voice even. "Not sure."

"The polite thing to do would be to give me your gate code and let me stay at the house. River's like a sister to me, and technically it's *her* house now, right? And Bear *is* a brother to me, and he'd want to know I was here and safe as soon as possible. Trust me, you don't want to pick a fight with him."

"See what I mean?" McCreedy added with an exasperated huff.

"I haven't seen him in weeks." Technically it had been ten days, but she didn't need that information.

"He wouldn't just abandon her."

"He didn't."

"So where is he?"

"Dunno. I'm not his keeper. He's a grown-ass man. For all I know, he could be on his way back home."

The lies burned in my throat. She deserved the truth, but not like this. Not over the phone, surrounded by strangers. We'd tell her once River was safe. Once my wife was back in my arms where she belonged. The last thing Gigi needed was to find out we'd buried her brother in an unmarked grave near the pond.

Bishop tried to put up a fight, said he should at least go to the morgue in case there was evidence that could be pulled and used in the case they were building against Volkov, but we vetoed that pretty quickly. A dead body raised too many questions we couldn't answer.

"I'm not leaving until I talk to them. River never ignores my calls. Do you have her chained up somewhere? She told me how much she hated you."

The accusation hit harder than she could have known, because while I wasn't the one who put her in chains, there was little doubt in my mind it was an accurate assessment of her current situation.

"Trust me, spitfire, if she was chained up anywhere on my land, she'd have begged for it."

"Spitfire. Oh, I like that," McCreedy mused.

"Don't even think about it, asshole," she shot back.

"Jackson, take me off speaker," I grumbled.

There was a soft rustle, muffled voices, and then he was back in my ear loud and clear. "Done."

"We've got a situation on our hands—"

"Plausible deniability!" he all but shouted at me.

"—so you need to do whatever you have to do to keep her away from the ranch. Take some time off, go visit that lake house of yours. I don't give a shit how you do it, just stay the fuck away from here. I'll call you when it's safe to bring her back."

McCreedy groaned. "You don't pay me enough for this."

"I pay you plenty. You could wipe your ass with your Christmas bonus from last year and still have more money than you could ever hope to spend."

"Consider this my official notice. My retainer for Cross Industries just doubled."

"Done."

"Shit, you really need me to handle this, don't you?"

"I wouldn't ask if I didn't."

We both sighed, silence stretching between us until I softly added, "That woman means a lot to my wife. Take care of her."

"You say woman, I say banshee." He sighed again. "I'll try. Seems more likely one of us will kill the other. I expect you to back me up when I plead self-defense."

"Plausible deniability," I said with a snicker, a smile stretching despite my black mood. It was rare I got to see my lawyer so flustered.

He wisely hung up before he said anything else that might land him on my shitlist.

Glancing at the clock, I cursed under my breath. I needed to clean up before my stupid fucking business dinner. I didn't have time for normal things like dinners with potential clients, but outwardly Cross Industries needed to look like the well-oiled machine we were supposed to be. One show of weakness and it'd be over. I couldn't lose everything my family had begged, borrowed, and stolen to get.

I trudged up the stairs, the weight of the last week making every step feel like a thousand. All I wanted to do was fall face-first into my bed, sleep for about a year, and wake up with River wrapped around me.

Thirty minutes later, I stood in front of my mirror, adjusting the sterling silver bolo tie my grandfather had given me when I'd turned eighteen. A soft rap at the door was my only warning before Walker peeked his head inside. Seeing I was dressed, he pushed it the rest of the way open and joined me, leaning heavily on his cane.

"Sorry you have to take this one tonight. I just don't think I can get through a whole damn dinner with my leg like this." His lips twitched up in a lopsided grin. "Not to mention they'd expect me to drink with them, and I don't think I should be in public mixing alcohol with these meds, fun though it might be. I'm liable to give away the fucking farm."

I let out a derisive snort. "Never stopped you before. That's how we lost Petunia."

Petunia was our prized bull. Yes, Petunia was male. Walker named him when he was three. No one had the heart to correct him, so Petunia it was—up until he lost him in an impromptu poker match after six rounds of tequila and his new owner renamed him Pete.

"Always throwing that in my face. I could argue you lost us Riv—" his face fell as he stopped himself, but it hurt just the same.

It was fucking true. I'd lost her a decade ago, and I didn't save her this time.

"That wasn't fair. I'm sorry, Cross. If anyone got her into this mess, it was her father. And ours," he added with a heavy sigh.

"No, you got it right the first time. This is on me. I let him get away with her."

"Dammit, stop playing the martyr. I can't hate you when you're all angsty and conciliatory like this. Takes all the fun out of it."

"I should have stopped him."

"He would have killed you."

"He should have. She would still be here with you if I'd just been man enough to rush him."

"You and I both know that's a lie. There was no way they were gonna stop until they got what they came for. They would have taken each and every one of us out to do it too. Us still being here means there's still a fighting chance."

I blinked at my brother, turning away from the mirror to face him fully. "Do you really believe that?"

"I have to, man. It's the only thing helping me get out of bed in the morning."

Heaving a sigh, I straightened the cuffs of my shirt before reaching for the blazer I'd hung on the back of a chair. "I hate that we have to pretend like everything's normal. Like she just up and left me."

Walk and I had decided that for the sake of appearances, when people asked about my new wife, I'd say she was packing up her house in Alaska and would be rejoining me as soon as she could. It excused her absence without creating any red flags, and it gave us a reason to not have a definitive return date.

But it would only last for so long. And it required Volkov to play ball. At any point, he could choose to present evidence proving me wrong. He was the one puppeteering this fucking game. I was the one out here with my ass flapping in the wind.

"They won't think that."

"They will if she isn't here soon."

"If she isn't here soon, we'll have bigger fish to fry. In the meantime, we gotta hope that Bishop's lead pans out and it's a moot point by this time next week."

I studied my younger brother. "I never realized you were such a cock-eyed optimist."

"Then you haven't been paying attention, brother. I'm optimistic as fuck. About the right things."

"We can't all be you. Some of us have to focus on getting shit done."

Walker clapped me on the shoulder. "You need to eat. You're hangry."

"What I need is my wife back."

"Right, and in the meantime, you should eat. Don't think I haven't noticed you've been skipping meals. You gotta stay in fighting shape, especially now. Never know when you're gonna have to face off with that fucker who stole her. Can't have you fainting when you need to be murdering."

"Walker, do you even hear half the shit that comes out of your mouth?"

He smirked, those blue eyes of his twinkling. "I do. It's sage wisdom."

"It's bullshit."

"One man's bullshit is another man's—"

"Bullshit."

"Even shit can be useful. Ever hear of fertilizer?"

"This conversation is over."

I slipped on the jacket, then grabbed my black Stetson and put it on, sighing as our father's face stared back at me. "I look like a fucking asshole."

"You are a fucking asshole."

I stared at him for a beat before a fleeting grin twisted at my lips. "Fair enough."

"If the Stetson fits, right?"

Huffing out a laugh, I nodded. "Suppose so."

"Next week, once the doc clears me, I'll be able to take these dinners off your plate. I'm almost ready to get out there again."

Given the state of his injuries, Walker really had recovered well. I'd thought it would take a lot longer to come back from the burns and broken leg, not to mention the rest of the damage, but due to his age and overall health, he'd made remarkable progress in only five weeks. It would be months before he was fully healed, but he'd be walking without pain any day now. Out of stubbornness, if nothing else. It didn't hurt that we had our own private doctor who gave him the best medical care money could buy.

The drugs helped too.

"Go secure this deal, get us some more beef, and then we'll keep looking for our wife."

I narrowed my eyes at him. "She's *my* wife. And I'm purchasing cattle, not beef."

"Same thing."

"Is not. You order beef at a restaurant."

"It's all beef in the end."

"You're a real philosopher, Walker."

My brother beamed at me. "Yes. Yes, I am. You know, that might be the nicest thing you've ever said to me."

"Don't get used to it."

We shared a smile that felt a lot less stilted than usual. In fact, ever since River came back—even with the discovery of our nuptials—Walker and I were closer than we'd ever been. Guess his almost dying twice had something to do with that. Or maybe it was just bonding over our feelings about the same woman. Either way, I wondered if this was how it'd be between us from now on. Camaraderie with him wasn't something I thought I'd ever have. I'd take it.

"See you when I get back," I said with a sharp nod.

"Call if you run into trouble."

"What are you gonna do, hobble to my rescue?"

"Ha ha. Very funny. Bishop's on standby. So's Tex."

"Let's hope I don't need them."

six

• • •

Bishop

Now that Volkov had made a move, it was more important than ever to keep Cross in my sights. Even if Walker hadn't asked me to tag along tonight, I'd have been here. I recognized the wild look in Cross's eyes—I'd worn the same expression more than once—the man was about to snap. That's why I was being choked by a damn tie and toying with the rim of my untouched whiskey glass as I sat in this fancy steak house a table away from him.

He hadn't noticed me. I'd been led in after him, and he had his back to me. The hope was we'd keep it that way. Neither of us could afford a public blowup if he decided he wanted me gone. Me for the obvious reasons, even though my cover was barely intact these days, but also because we were trying to keep things about River under wraps. We'd all agreed it was safest for her that way.

Unfortunately, hotheads were all the same. Unpredictable.

That went for the Russian as well as Cross. There was no telling what those two were liable to do, which made me twitchy.

How was I supposed to keep anyone safe when the only thing I could predict with any certainty was trouble?

Cross shifted in his chair, an irritated sigh escaping him as he glanced at his watch.

"Fucking ten minutes late, you bastard. I don't have time for this," he muttered, so low I almost couldn't make it out.

He pulled out his phone and tapped at the screen. I glanced down at mine, clearly seeing the message he was typing thanks to the software my buddy helped me install on the sly. One click on a discreet little app icon, and his phone was completely mirrored on my screen. There'd be hell to pay if he ever found out.

CROSS:

Is this guy always fucking late?

WALKER:

Ted? Yeah, usually by a few minutes.

CROSS:

If he's not here in five, I'm calling it and the deal is off the table.

WALKER:

Fair.

Without warning, he closed his messages and clicked on his photo gallery. Dozens of images of River filled the screen, and my hand tightened reflexively on my phone. Cross chose one at random—so far as I could tell anyway—and her smiling face peered back at me.

Holy fuck, I missed her.

It'd been two weeks, and already it felt like something vital within me had been lost.

Sterling was long gone, replaced by the unfeeling and soulless shell of a man I'd been in the days following my rescue. I was in survival mode, doing any and everything I could to pass the time while waiting to get her back.

All that mattered was the mission.

Cross's phone went black, and my attention shot back to the scene in real time. He'd gotten to his feet, slipping his cell into the breast pocket of his blazer. A tall man with a thick mustache approached, a wide smile on his face and one hand resting on the hip of his companion, a statuesque Black woman with curves that rivaled a back road. I raised an eyebrow at the way he looked at her as he held out her chair. Sonofabitch had a solid reason for being late.

"Sorry I'm late, Daniel. Tracy had some trouble with her dress." Ted offered a hand, but Cross didn't shake.

"Call me Cross. Daniel was my father, and I'd like it to stay that way."

"Oh, sure thing, Cross. I get it. I'm named after my granddaddy, but I never wanted to be called Theodore."

"Although he lets me get away with Teddy every once in a while," Tracy said with a stunning smile.

I wouldn't be surprised to learn the woman graced the pages of fashion magazines. How the hell *Ted* managed to score her was a mystery for the ages.

Cross must have thought the same, though he didn't offer more than a soft grunt.

"So where's your lady wife? I told Tracy this was a double date. Husbands talk shop, wives talk . . . whatever they want." Ted smiled, stepping right in it with no fucking idea it was the worst possible question he could ask.

Cross's shoulders stiffened, climbing up around his ears, and as I watched, he tucked his hands into his lap, curling them into tight fists to mask the trembling of his fingers. "Away."

Ted cocked one brow. "Already? You a snorer? I'll tell you a secret, invest in a solid set of earplugs for her, or even better, I got Tracy a headband with little speakers in it. She listens to her audiobooks, and I can snore away."

"Well, aren't you just a fucking delight?" Cross grumbled before raising his hand and signaling for service.

"Was it something I said?" Ted asked softly, his voice only just reaching me as he angled his head toward his woman.

She soothingly ran a hand over his chest, shaking her head slightly. "Think you touched a nerve, babe." She gave him a sweet kiss. "I wouldn't worry about it. Cross here has a bit of a reputation for being a jackass."

I had to bite back a smile at her assessment. The censure in her words was unmistakable. Cross better watch out. She was liable to come after him if he spoke out of turn about her husband. Something about the entire exchange made me think of River, and just that quick, my smile fell, my heart giving a dejected little pang.

The waitress bounded over, hearts in her eyes for the broody cowboy who'd summoned her. "What can I get you, Mr. Cross? Another of the same?"

"Yes, and whatever they're having."

"Nothing fancy for me, just an Arnold Palmer, thanks. I'm responsible for driving this pretty lady home." Ted tilted his head toward his wife. "You want the usual, babe?" Tracy nodded, so he continued chattering at the server, "A glass of your finest Pinot Gris, please." Then he chuckled. "Never gets old. I do love me a rhyme."

Cross had to be in agony. He was the grumpy to this man's sunshine. A match made straight in hell. I, however, was in heaven. This was way more entertaining than I could have ever hoped, and damn if I hadn't needed some levity.

"So, how's it been since your daddy handed you the reins? You holding up okay?" Ted asked.

Coming from anyone else, this could have been considered a dig or prying. But this man radiated genuine concern. He was like a golden retriever that just wanted you to pet his soft underbelly. If I wasn't witnessing it with my own eyes, I'd never believe a person could be this kind without any sort of agenda.

The man was the human equivalent of a hug. The sliver of my soul that was still untainted decided then and there he needed to be protected at all costs.

"Why wouldn't I be?" Cross bit out, accepting his fresh drink with barely more than a nod of thanks to the waitress.

"Well, losing him, gaining your wife, Walker getting hurt so bad in that tractor accident . . . It's enough to shake anyone. I guess I just wanted to make sure you were all right. I know when my own dad died, I tried real hard to pretend I was fine, but it ate me up inside. If not for Tracy here, I'd still be a blubbering mess."

Cross shook his head, as if he couldn't believe a grown man would admit such a thing—at a business dinner, of all places. But I could see

Ted was starting to wear him down. He released a breath and relaxed slightly.

"Yeah. It's been a lot."

Ted leaned forward, as if waiting for the rest of the confession. But it wasn't coming. Cross wouldn't air his dirty laundry even if he owned the damn laundromat. He was as tight-lipped as they came. Especially when it came to his family.

Or his feelings.

The only person he seemed to let his walls down for was River.

"You'll be okay. Eventually."

Cross cleared his throat, leaning back and taking a sip of his drink, then said, "We're not here to talk about personal things. Walker said you have an investment opportunity for us. Hit me with your best shot."

Ted lit up like a kid in a candy store as he dove into his pitch, but I was willing to bet Cross didn't hear a single word. Because none other than Dominik fucking Volkov chose that exact second to walk into the restaurant. His eyes lasered in on Cross, as if he'd known exactly where he'd be sitting, and his lips twisted up in a knowing smirk.

Shit.

This was no freak coincidence. That asshole was making a power play right here in front of half the upper-class members of this community. Most of them entangled with his organization in one form or another, even if they didn't realize it. On instinct, I touched the gun holstered at my side.

This was going to get messy. Fast.

I had to get Cross out of here.

And then I needed to figure out how to put a tail on Volkov without getting myself killed.

Our lead had turned out to be a dead end. Seeing the man here, in the flesh, told me he'd probably had that lead planted. He was onto us. Not just Cross, but the agents looking into him.

Motherfucker.

Before I could anticipate it, Cross shoved his chair back so hard it fell to the floor with a crash.

"Where is she, you prick? Where are you hiding her?" he shouted, two hundred plus pounds of enraged alpha male as he made to lunge across the table at the monster who'd stolen our woman.

I was behind him in an instant, one arm around his chest, restraining him. Cross struggled against my hold as Volkov let out a patronizing laugh.

"Lost your wife already, Cross? So much for a happy couple."

"I swear to God, if you hurt her, I will rain hell down on you tenfold."

Volkov laughed, a deep rumbling chuckle that only incensed Cross further.

Ted watched this all unfold with wide eyes, his body protectively placed in front of his wife, who I'd clocked when she palmed a steak knife from the table.

"Not here, Cross," I whispered. "You have to let him go right now."

He continued to fight my hold. "Like hell I will, that bastard—"

"I know exactly what that bastard has done. But this is what he wants. If you attack him here, he wins. There's more than a dozen witnesses that will claim you went after him unprovoked. You'll get thrown in jail for assault, and you're useless to her there."

"Unprovoked?" he spat.

"No one else knows he has River. To them, it will look like you were the one who started it."

Cross growled but backed down. "I'm good. Let me go."

I stepped away but kept myself close enough that I could stop him if Volkov tried another dig, but the big Russian had already walked away, taking a seat in a corner booth with a self satisfied grin.

"Come on, let's get out of here. None of this is helping our girl." I clapped him on the shoulder and prayed he'd see reason. Everything in me wanted to pummel Volkov until he talked, just like Cross, but I knew it wouldn't do any good.

Cross gave a tight nod, pulling out his wallet and dropping a couple hundreds on the table. "Apologies, but I need to cut our meeting short. Please enjoy dinner on me. I'll have my assistant follow up to reschedule."

Ted nodded, smoothing out his tie as he settled back in his seat. "Good call. Tensions are running a mite high at the moment. Best to regroup and chat when we can both focus. You just go relax. I'm not going anywhere."

It took me two tries, but Cross followed me out of the restaurant, both of us vibrating with adrenaline. When we hit the parking lot, he turned to me, anguish on his face.

"We have to get her back, Bishop. That fucker is taunting us. He doesn't think we'll beat him."

"We will."

"How?"

I shook my head, understanding the quiet devastation better than he knew. "Patience. Strategy. Backup. All things we don't have right now."

"And you don't care that he's probably done horrible things to her? Because every fucking minute that passes means he has another chance to hurt her."

Grabbing him by the collar, I shoved him against the side of his truck. "Never say that to me again. I'm doing what you seem to be unable to—searching for her, planning her rescue. We will find her. You have to trust me."

"Why should I trust you? You've been lying to me from day one, and your promises don't mean shit. Your leads are garbage. Your contacts can't find anything. What the fuck good are you, Bishop? From where I'm sitting, you're just letting him take her all over again. Whose side are you really on? It's like you want him to get away with it."

Finally at the end of my rope, I reared back and decked the fucker as hard as I could. Then, before he could get his bearings, I turned and walked to my waiting SUV. I didn't have time to fight with Cross in a parking lot. If he wanted to take on the entire Russian mob in a steak-house on his own, so be it. I had a call to make, information to uncover, and a woman to save.

Because despite his baseless accusations, the only side I'd ever been on was hers.

seven

• • •

Walker

Blue nudged me as I stood near her stall, begging for the sugar cubes I'd stashed in my pocket. My leg ached from how long I'd been on my feet today, but I wouldn't baby myself any longer. I needed to be as close to one hundred percent as possible before we got River back.

"Impatient, huh? You don't even really want to see me. You're only in it for the sweets," I told the horse, but I held out my palm, sugar cubes in the center. She snubbed me, refusing to take my offering. "I beg your pardon. This is your favorite."

"She's mad at you. You've been gone too long," Tex said, striding out of the tack room with a smirk on his face. "I've been taking care of her for you."

"Moving in on my best girl, huh?"

"Someone had to make sure she had attention."

I stroked the side of her neck, chuckling to myself as I realized horses were no better than most of the women I'd dated. They were just as needy and vindictive, if not more so. It was a small mercy they couldn't speak, or text, for that matter. Pretty sure Blue would have blown my phone up with her demands otherwise.

"I sure do have a type, don't I?" I muttered.

Except River wasn't like that. She was complicated, sure, but she'd never been any of those other things toward me.

"Where's the boss lady been? Trouble in paradise?" Tex asked, making the hair on the back of my neck stand on end.

"She's just taking care of something back in Alaska. She'll be home soon."

Tex's brows raised. "I thought she was supposed to stay here for a year or risk the ranch going up for auction."

Fuck. I'd forgotten about that. Senior's bullshit stipulations didn't seem all that important in the wake of River's kidnapping. But to the folks on the ranch, it was their livelihoods at stake. It would sure as shit matter to them.

"Since this was an emergency, the three of us agreed in writing that her leaving would have no bearing on that."

Tex lifted his hat and scratched at his head. "You can do that?"

I let out a laugh that I was pretty sure sounded as fake as it felt. "Oh, sure. You can do anything so long as a lawyer drafts it up and makes it sound pretty."

"Well, she'd better get back here soon. There's been rumblings, and her absence has been noticed."

Narrowing my eyes, I asked, "Rumblings? What kind of rumblings?"

Tex leaned back against the stable wall, pulling his phone from his pocket as he did. "Like this, for instance. Not even an hour ago, the gossip mill started posting online about your sad brother being left by his new bride."

He shoved the device at me, and I stared down at a photo of a frowning Cross at dinner tonight, alone with an untouched glass of whiskey. Sure, the man was almost always frowning, but this time he looked . . . haggard.

Not sure what to say to that, I laughed it off. "You set up a Google alert or something, super spy?"

Tex shrugged and pocketed his phone. "I like to stay in the know when it comes to the ranch, and since you and your brother *are* the ranch . . ."

"Fair 'nuff."

A twist of anxiety in my gut had me itching to bring out my own phone and scroll through every last post that mentioned us. But I also knew that wouldn't do anything to bring River back to us.

"She'll be back soon. Any day now."

"Good. I wouldn't want to lose my job just because Cross can't hold on to his wife."

I was hit with the unfamiliar need to defend my brother. Usually I was the first to shove his sorry ass under the bus. But things between us had started to mend. Lately it didn't feel like we were adversaries so much as, well, brothers.

"You might do best to watch your mouth, Tex."

He straightened and cleared his throat. "Roger that. Didn't mean nothing by it, just thought you should know the boys are worried and see if there was anything I could pass on that might soothe some ruffled feathers."

"Everything's fine," I spat, knowing on the inside absolutely nothing was.

Blue took that moment to nudge my shoulder so hard I nearly lost my balance, but I was thankful for the distraction. I needed something to break the tension between Tex and I. Offering her the sugar once more, I sighed when she finally took it.

A car door slamming from outside caught my attention, followed by a second and then indecipherable but definitely raised voices.

Tex craned his neck, looking toward the ruckus. "Seems like Cross is on a tear. If it's all the same to you, I'll make myself scarce."

Unfortunately, I couldn't do the same. He needed to know that the media had caught on to River's disappearance and were posting about it. Good thing he was already in a foul mood, because I was about to make it worse.

Using my cane, I moved as fast as I could through the stable, cursing my injuries because they slowed me down. I heard them as soon as I got inside the house, Cross shouting and Bishop's calm responses. My brother's volume rose with every step I took toward them.

"I should fucking fire you," Cross growled.

"You should put some ice on that."

I moved into the room right as my brother snarled and raised his fist like he was about to take a swing. "What the fuck is going on?"

Cross spun toward me, and I clocked his face. "Ouch," I winced, noting how the skin beneath his eye was already an angry red moving toward purple and guessing it wouldn't be long before the eye was swollen shut. "You really *should* put some ice on that. Or peas. Maybe a steak."

"Fuck off, Walker. No one asked you."

I gestured toward my cane. "I'm sort of the resident expert on the subject these days. Maybe you should ask me."

Cross grunted and shook his head, returning to the whiskey he'd been pouring into a glass before Bishop goaded him into a reaction.

"So, which one of you is going to tell me how that happened? There's no way Ted did it. The man's a pussycat."

"I punched him," Bishop said, no shame in his words whatsoever.

If looks could kill, the glare my brother shot Bishop would have had him bleeding out all over the floor. I, however, found the situation amusing as hell.

"You're not the first. Doubt you'll be the last. What he do this time?"

Cross's grip was tight enough on his glass I worried he'd break it. "Not a damn thing. That's the fucking problem."

"I'm not following."

"Volkov was there. He was trying to get Cross to step out of line."

My eyes widened, anger surging through me at the bastard's name. "Why the fuck would he do that? Why now?"

My brother sighed. "It was a blatant power move. He wanted us to know we couldn't touch him. Except, I could have shot him right between the eyes then and there."

Bishop snorted. "And then your ass would be in jail, and we'd be no closer to getting River back."

A vein bulged in Cross's neck, his jaw clenched so hard I could practically hear his teeth grinding. "Which is the only reason that motherfucker is still breathing."

I released a breath I hadn't realized I was holding, hating that the explanation made sense. Then I immediately tensed again, remembering I still had news of my own to share.

"Well, we've got other problems too. The ranch hands are getting antsy. They've noticed River is gone, and so has pretty much all of Devil's Grove. If we don't get her back soon, it's gonna be hard to keep the property in our hands. We'll lose everything, her included."

Bishop crossed his arms over his chest, focusing on the empty fireplace. "And Volkov will swoop in and steal this place from under you."

"I bet that asshole is behind the press catching wind of it," Cross grumbled. "Even though he's the one who took her, he's the one who benefits the most from people knowing."

Goddammit, the Russian was a slippery sonofabitch. "Course he's behind it. As soon as people find out the stipulations Senior set forth in the will have been breached, he'll get everything he wants. And the press didn't do us any favors when they practically published the will like it was a damn novel."

"Goddamn public record. No one cares unless there's gossip to be had." Bishop's low rumble was more to himself than us.

"Or you're Volkov, looking for a way to fuck us over," I said, one thing becoming increasingly clear as we discussed our current predicament.

Dominik had planned all of it. Not just the kidnapping, but how to use the will against us. It would have been impressive if it wasn't our lives he was fucking with. If it wasn't our woman he was hurting.

Bishop's phone rang, and to my surprise, he answered, excusing himself from the room and leaving the two of us to wallow.

"I fucking hate this. Volkov has us hamstrung. Dad would be ashamed to see us like this," I muttered.

Cross dragged a hand through his hair. "What do you want from me? I've shut down their ability to ship with us, cut them off, and would've killed the asshole if Bishop hadn't stopped me. What else can I do? Buy off the damn papers? For every one I silence, three more pop up. Not to mention the social media posts from people in town."

His frustration mirrored my own. "I don't know, but we need to do something. I can't just sit around waiting for Dom to make his next move. It's time we start making moves of our own. I mean, fuck, we're the sons of Daniel Cross. If anyone knows about making moves, it's us. We all but cut our teeth on Senior's mind fuckery."

A smirk twisted Bishop's lips as he rejoined us. "I think I have an idea. As long as you're up for some shady shit."

I laughed. "And you call yourself a special agent. It's like you don't know us at all. Shady shit is our bread and butter. Hell, I'm pretty sure it's coded into our DNA or, at the very least, the heart of our family motto."

Cross gave an exasperated huff, stopping me before my ramble went any further. "Go ahead, Bishop. We're listening."

eight

. . .

River

My limbs trembled involuntarily as I sat huddled in the corner, shivering, clammy, but lucid. I hadn't been this aware of my surroundings since I arrived here. They'd kept me drugged pretty consistently. Until now.

Time was an absolutely foreign concept. It could have been weeks or months; everything was a hazy blur. All I knew for certain was the door to my cell would eventually open, and a guard would come in with my meal. It was the only time the door ever opened, meaning it was my only chance to escape.

As if summoned by my thoughts, the faint sound of footsteps filtered from under the door, the telltale jangle of keys and guard number three's incessant whistling following shortly after. I tensed as my mind whirled with every possible choice I had.

The thought of leaving this room filled my veins with spiders made from fear. I didn't know what waited for me beyond it. Freedom, hopefully. But it could just as easily be an entire army of my enemies. I could barely stand upright on my own. How could I run? Fight? They didn't even give me plastic utensils to eat with. I had almost nothing at my disposal.

Although this time . . . this time I had a fully functioning brain.

That was a hell of a lot more than what I'd been operating on. They seriously fucked up when they left me lucid. Either they underestimated my will to live, or they weren't used to their prisoners fighting back. If that was the case, they'd have to kill me first, because I would fight with every last breath in my body.

The lack of weapons in this room put me at a severe disadvantage. But I was resourceful. I'd use my nails and teeth. I'd kick and punch until I couldn't anymore. Technically, I also had a bucket of shit. Not bad as far as weapons went.

These monsters drugged me and made me live in my own filth for God knows how long. Maybe it was time I turned the tables. Tried a little biological warfare of my own.

Listening hard for the footsteps, I scrambled to the other side of my cramped quarters and picked up the little bucket that had served as my toilet. I gritted my teeth against the wave of nausea that threatened, telling myself it was no worse than mucking stalls. Except horseshit was a lot fucking different than this.

"Come on, you bastard. I've got something for you." My voice was rusty with disuse, barely more than a whisper, but I drew strength from my threat all the same.

The door opened, revealing the guard I'd been expecting, his youthful face and white-blond hair making him appear sweet and innocent. I knew better. He might be the smallest of them, but he was terrifying in his cruelty.

"Hello there, shlyukha. How nice to see you on your feet for once."

He didn't have a tray with him, so it must not be mealtime. Which meant they had other plans for me.

My heart lurched, adrenaline flooding my system and helping me find strength. I only had one shot at this. I couldn't let him get his hands on me, or I'd be overpowered and out of the game before it even really started.

"Fuck you, you piece of shit," I growled—or tried to—before flinging the contents of the bucket straight at his face and then lobbing the bit of metal at him for good measure.

Instinctively, he gagged and coughed, bending at the waist as he worked to get control of himself. That was all I needed. I darted as fast as my weakened muscles allowed, escaping his blindly reaching arms and making it to the open door. Thank God he'd been careless and hadn't locked it behind him.

I'd love to say I tapped into some long dormant track star hidden within me and sprinted down the hallway. But it was less sprint and more graceless stumble. I fell almost immediately and had to crawl back up to my feet, using the wall to help keep me upright as I staggered forward.

Just keep going, River.

I had seconds at most before he recovered from my shit shower and called for reinforcements. They'd kill me if they caught me.

An enraged bellow sounded behind me, and I tried to push myself faster. Panic had a sob building in my chest, but I couldn't release the cry and waste precious energy.

Blinding pain burned from the roots of my hair, spreading across my scalp as I was hauled backward. The stench of my urine radiated off him with every step he took.

"Fucking cunt. We should have just killed you. Done the world a favor."

Even through my pain, my brain caught onto his words.

"Why didn't you?" I spat.

"Because at the moment, you're worth more alive than dead."

He had no idea how much he'd just given away with that statement. If they needed me alive, that gave me a world of leeway. I swung my arm down, aiming for his dick, but not quite sure what I made contact with.

He snarled in response, shoving me back to my corner. "Don't move."

"Fuck you." I launched myself at him again, ready to tear into him. In my mind, I was a fierce combination of football player and MMA fighter. In reality, I was probably a more pathetic version of a kitten.

Bear would be so disappointed in my form, but he'd be proud as hell of my fight.

My heart gave a pang at the thought of my protector and the pool of blood he'd been lying in when I last saw him.

I let out an enraged cry, hating these monsters who had taken so much more from me than they could ever know. I lashed out, nails raking across the motherfucker's skin. It must have hurt because he backhanded me, the blow hard enough my vision went fuzzy, and pain immediately blossomed in my cheek.

I fell to the floor, my head swimming as he raised a booted foot.

Oh God. He might've said I was worth more alive than dead, but he was all fury and contempt. And there was a whole world of possibility between alive and dead. He never said what state I needed to be in. Broken was still technically alive. So was catatonic.

Fuck.

I closed my eyes, waiting for the moment he brought that foot down, praying the strike to my face would send me into unconsciousness before I had to endure the pain he was going to dole out.

The harsh boom of a gunshot made me flinch just before the spray of something warm peppered my skin. I wanted to open my eyes. See who rescued me from this asshole. But the shock and fatigue were too much, and everything around me faded into oblivion.

WHEN I CAME TO, my face felt as if it belonged to a bobblehead. It was swollen and way heavier than usual. One eye was all I could open, and every movement of my cheek sent a deep ache through my muscles as I worked to focus on my surroundings.

"Shit. What happened? How long have I been out?" I whispered, knowing it would be one of my three men at my side.

Who else would have come to my rescue and shot my jailer?

Rough fingers gripped my chin and pulled my head to the side, where I saw the blond man had a massive hole where his face used to be. "Look what you made me do. Alexsei was such a promising young man, and now he's dead because he lost his temper."

Fear raced through every cell, my body trembling in response to the sound of my kidnapper's voice. "Th-thanks for the r-rescue. Get your f-fucking hands off me."

"Oh, malyshka, I didn't rescue you. I'm protecting Dominik's investment."

"W-what?"

He grinned, and that might have been the most terrifying thing of all. "You're going to auction, pretty bird." He laughed at the horror he must have read in my expression. "That's right. Time to earn your keep."

He grabbed me by the arm and hauled me up, a desperate whimper leaving me at the cruel treatment.

"Take off your clothes. We need to get you cleaned up for the auction. With a body like yours, no one will care what your face looks like. They'll still pay top dollar."

"For what?" I managed, but deep down, I knew.

"To own you."

nine

. . .

Bishop

I shut the shower off with a heavy sigh, hating this limbo we were living in. I should be used to it, and in a way, I was. Undercover work was a frustrating combination of hurry up and wait. But the missions I'd used to lead as a SEAL were much more action-oriented. We were the guys you called in once you'd gathered all the intelligence. We were the ones who got shit done.

I much preferred those days to this. Especially right now, where my woman was the central piece of my new mission. Everything else had been abandoned. She was the only thing that mattered now. And I couldn't do anything until we had more intel.

As I toweled off, using far more force than necessary, I fought the urge to take action, make some kind of move forward. But what could I do? Ride my horse down Main Street and call her name like a lovesick fool?

I'd put out feelers, reached out to contacts I hadn't talked to in years, and in a desperate bid for progress, even called in a favor from a hacker I knew. So far, it'd been radio silence on all fronts since my last break.

"Asher, come on. I know you're better than this," I muttered, opening the email app on my phone and refreshing my inbox over and over.

I was about to throw my phone against the wall in a rage when a new message appeared from Black Hat Industries.

"Thank fuck."

My heart was a wild thing in my chest as I opened the email and read.

To: Sterling__Bishop@contactme.com
From: YoureWelcome@BHI.com
Subject: What kinda shit are you into?

Facial recognition pinged on your mark. Take a look. All the info I could get is below via an encrypted link. DO NOT open this on a regular fucking browser.

Good luck. Now leave me the fuck alone. I've had enough crises on my plate for the rest of my life. I don't need to borrow yours.

A

PS: Please tell me you're gonna take care of the motherfucker who's responsible for this.

AT THE VERY BOTTOM of his email, there was a subscript so small it was nearly illegible.

In lieu of payment, if you'd like to adopt a puffin and make a donation to Savepuffins.org, I'll consider us square. If you're an asshole with no heart, you can click this link and pay your invoice.

"Puffins? Who the fuck likes puffins that much?" I muttered, but all questions dried up on my tongue as soon as I clicked the encrypted link in the body of his email.

She was there. Standing directly in front of the camera, eyes haunted, face gaunt, looking painfully beautiful, even scared as she was.

Ice filled my veins when I realized what this picture was for. My hands shook as I dragged on a pair of sweats and stormed out of my room, shouting for Cross as I descended the stairs.

I found him in the office, seated behind the desk while Walker and Tex sat opposite each other near the fireplace. They all looked my way when I stormed in.

"We've got a problem," I said without preamble, casting a dark look at Tex. "Leave."

His brows lifted. "Are you the boss? Anything *you* have to say, you can say in front of me."

"You heard him," Cross growled.

"How'd the new guy get so far up your ass?" Tex demanded.

"He saved my life. Twice," Walker said, matching his brother's stormy countenance.

"Well fuck me running. I guess my years of loyalty don't mean shit in the face of that."

I stared him down, frustrated as hell that he was ignoring our orders for him to leave. "Get out or I'll make you."

The cowboy stood, his jaw clenched. "Just because you're fucking Miss Adams, that doesn't mean you can skip your way up the chain of command."

"That's enough, Tex. You keep River's name out of your mouth," Cross snapped, shoving his chair back and bracing his palms on the desk.

"He's her bodyguard," Walker offered. Not technically the truth, but it gave Tex a solid reason to shut the fuck up.

The ranch hand adjusted his hat and sniffed, giving the Cross brothers a jerk of his head. "I suppose we'll continue planning our next run when Bishop here finishes sharing whatever was so important he had to barge in here uninvited. Excuse me, y'all."

As soon as he was gone, Cross approached, his disapproving glare trained on my chest. "You own a shirt?"

"It was too important to waste time. You're lucky I put on pants."

"What's going on?" Walker asked.

Pulling my phone out and bringing up the email from Asher, I opened the link again. "I found her."

Cross snatched my phone before the page had fully populated, eyes wild, breaths dragging in and out as he took in River. I knew what he'd see, and I hated it.

The way the heavy makeup she'd never apply herself did nothing to hide the swelling of her cheek. How the sorry excuse of a dress that clung to her sweet curves was all wrong. As were the shadows in her dull green eyes and the gauntness in her face. Nothing about the woman in the picture conveyed River's fierce spirit. They'd broken her, and it was our fault for taking so damn long to find her.

"What the fuck is this?" Cross snarled.

"An auction listing. Volkov's selling her, just like we thought."

Walker got to shaky feet and hobbled over, staring at the photo with rapidly growing ire in his expression. "That motherfucker. When I get my hands on him, I'll geld him myself and bronze his balls. Then maybe beat him over the head with them for good measure."

"You'll get your chance," I grunted. "After me."

"How do we stop this?" Walker asked.

I opened my mouth, but Cross beat me to answering.

"We buy her back."

"What? How's that gonna work? Dom's not exactly going to let the three of us waltz on in his little party."

"It's anonymous," I told him, sharing some of the intel Wilson had learned about the infamous auctions. "The attendees are all masked to protect themselves. Cash payments only. No names. No bank accounts. Nothing traceable."

"So we go in there, pay top dollar for our girl, and then just leave with her?" Walker asked. "Sounds too easy."

"No. *I* go in there. You don't do a damn thing." Cross raked a hand through his hair, frustration leaching out of him.

"This is fucking bullshit. I've been forced on the sidelines for all of this. She's my girl as much as she is yours. I need to do something to save her."

"You're gonna drive the car."

He glared at his brother and gestured to his body and the cane leaning against the table. "What about me screams getaway driver to you? I'm *barely* walking. You want me stomping on gas pedals now?"

"If River isn't enough motivation—"

"I didn't fucking say that. Don't put words in my mouth. I just think out of the two of us, you might be the better choice."

"I could do it," I offered.

"Drive?" Walker asked.

"Go to the auction. Be the bidder."

Cross's fingers tightened on my phone, his posture even more rigid than normal. "I'm going in. End of story. It's gotta be me."

"It's always you. Every fucking time. You think you'll ride in on your white horse and rescue her so she'll fall in love with you again. God, you're pathetic."

Dragging in a ragged breath, Cross said, "No. It has to be me because your limp will give you away and make you a liability. Captain America here will stand out like a sore thumb. But me? I belong with these assholes. I'm the slimiest snake in this house." He paused as though gathering his words, then with a break in his voice, offered his darkest confession. "Besides . . . I was the one who lost her. No one else is responsible for that." He sighed, handing me back the phone. "Don't you fucking get it? I have to be the one to bring her home because it's the only way I can live with myself."

Walker rubbed a hand down the back of his neck. "And then what? He's going to realize we're the ones who got her when she just shows back up here. What's gonna stop him from coming after her again?"

He had a point. A damn good one. If I couldn't put Volkov and his minions behind bars, we'd be in a world of hurt. But Cross shook his head, striding over to the bar cart in the corner and pouring a healthy glass of scotch.

"Me," Cross growled, looking every inch the ruthless bastard I knew him to be before he knocked back his drink.

Sensing what he was about to say, I opened my mouth to stop him. Anything he said in front of me could be used against him. He shouldn't incriminate himself; I was duty-bound to testify against him.

But he looked me dead in the eye, all but daring me to stop him as he vowed, "The next time I see that motherfucker, I'm gonna kill him."

ten

. . .

Cross

"Pick up the phone, you bastard," I growled as I paced back and forth in my room.

What the fuck was McCreedy doing that kept him from answering my calls? There shouldn't be a damn thing aside from death or incapacitation that sent me to fucking voicemail. But I'd called twice now.

Twice.

Both times ended with me hanging up when his automated greeting kicked in.

"You better be fucking dying, asshole."

I hit the call button a third time, already thinking through how I could get out of our contract and fire his ass if he didn't answer. It would be a shame. His family had worked with mine a long time, and I considered him a friend, but River's life was on the line. I couldn't have her wasting away while he sat around with his dick in his hand.

"Cross . . . what's . . . up?" His heaving breaths between each word said he'd been running . . . or fucking. Hell.

"Where the good goddamn were you?"

"Dealing with . . . the . . . demon you saddled me with."

"She can't be that bad."

He huffed. "She's a fucking . . . hellcat."

I pinched the bridge of my nose. "Please tell me you aren't fucking her."

There was a slight pause. "Don't ask questions you don't want answers to."

Fuck.

"Jackson . . ."

Clearing his throat, he said, "What can I do for you, Cross?"

Bishop's words echoed in my mind as I recalled the intense conversation we had before I made this call.

"How much should I be prepared to spend?"

Bishop sat down on the couch and sighed. "We've seen girls go for half a mil, easy."

"Then we'll have a million ready," Walker said. "Can we get that much?"

I wasn't sure, but we'd have to. It wasn't so much a matter of money as time. Liquidating that many assets in a day or two would be tricky. "I'll call McCreedy, see what can be done on short notice."

"Sell Dad's cars. As many as you need to. I don't want 'em if she's not here."

My chest ached at the thought of her not coming home. Walker and I were of one mind. Money was nothing. We'd live in a shack as long as we had her. Rising from my chair, I gave the two of them a tight nod and headed to my room so I could make my call.

McCreedy said my name again, pulling me back from the memory. Swallowing through a thick throat, I said, "I need you to get me a million dollars by tomorrow. Cash."

He laughed. "You're hilarious."

"I'm serious."

"This is about"—there was a beat of silence where I could easily picture him checking to make sure he was alone—"*her*, isn't it?"

"Yes."

He blew out a breath. "I mean, if we were talking wire transfer, no problem. If you want me to hand you a suitcase filled with cash, that's going to take some time."

"We don't have time. We have a day. And you're wasting it."

"Jesus, Cross."

Remembering what Walker said, I added, "Oh, do you still have that guy's name? The one who wanted to buy Hades?"

"Uh, yeah. Stuart something. I'm sure I can find it."

"Call him. Tell him if he can pay in cash today, the horse is his."

McCreedy whistled softly. "You serious, Cross? You love that horse."

"Not as much as I love her." I wasn't ever gonna shy away from the truth about how deep my feelings ran for my wife again. She'd gone too many years thinking she meant nothing to me. From now on, every fucking person on this earth would know she was my everything. There wasn't another option.

"And the asking price?"

"A hundred grand. No negotiation."

He sighed. "I'll see what I can do."

"No. You'll do it, or don't show your face in town again."

"I'll call you when it's done."

"A million. I mean it. And if you can't get it in cash, get creative. Pink slips. Items from the family vault. Anything to make up the difference."

"You're gonna trade in your mama's jewels?"

"I will hand over every fucking thing I have if it means I get her back in one piece. Do you hear me? Every. Fucking. Thing. Now make it happen, Jackson. I'm counting on you. No, fuck that. She's counting on you."

Was it fair to put the weight of our mess on him? No, but I didn't care. If it was the only way for him to do what needed to be done, I'd use every dirty trick in the book. This was her life on the line. Nothing was off limits.

Not even Mama's ring. The priceless piece of jewelry flashed in my mind, and a pang of loss hit me hard. River should be wearing it, but if we had to, we'd sell it too. It might be the last piece I let go of, but we'd sell all of it.

After a longer than usual pause, McCreedy replied, "Okay. I'm on it." His tone had a somber edge to it now. He understood the gravity of my situation and had shifted from beleaguered lawyer to loyal friend.

"Thank you."

I hung up just as a female voice filtered to my ears from the other end of the phone, and I simply had to trust Jackson not to fill River's friend in on our situation. Gigi wasn't going to be any help right now, but once we got River back, I had a feeling she'd be invaluable.

I WAS on pins and needles as I waited for Jackson to come through our front door the day after I'd called him. He'd buzzed for entry at the gate, and now it was only a matter of minutes before we had what we needed. We had three hours until the auction, and every passing second without a call from him had spun me tighter than a rattler coiled and ready to strike.

"Calm down, Cross. You're like a damn lion in a cage over there. He's comin'. We're fine," Walker said, but his shoulders were tight, eyes betraying his own stress. If not for the cane, he'd likely be pacing right alongside me.

The second Jackson's Aston Martin came to a stop, I was out the door and moving toward him. There was no missing his passenger, the pretty brunette's hair flying wildly around her thanks to the convertible's top being down.

"You've gotta be fucking shitting me," I gritted out under my breath.

Gigi—because that would be the only woman he'd be bold enough to bring with him—clutched the leather bag in her arms like it was a lifeline.

"Get out of the damn car, Virginia," Jackson barked.

"Go to hell, jackwad."

"I'm already there, hellcat," he growled. "Have been since the day you showed up in my office."

I smirked despite myself. In any other situation, this would be entertainment at its finest.

"Did you seriously bring a date to a business meeting?" Walker asked from behind me.

"Is that what we're calling this?" Gigi asked. "Is it normal to bring bags full of cash to"—she loosened her death grip on the bag just long enough to make elaborate finger quotes—"business meetings?"

"Damn, now we have to kill her," Walker murmured.

Her eyes widened, but to her credit, she didn't back down. "I'd like to see you try."

"Don't make any sudden moves, boys. She's unhinged. She grabbed the bag and wouldn't let go. That's the only reason she's here." McCreedy looked so harried I almost felt a twinge of sympathy for the man.

I'd never seen him this out of sorts in my life. Woman clearly had him by the balls. I hope she led him on a merry chase. *After* we got River back.

"All right, spitfire. Hand it over," I said as she got out of the convertible. "It's important. River needs it."

Narrowing her eyes, she asked, "River? Why would she need this much money? Isn't she like a gazillionaire now?"

Christ, this was a minefield. I didn't see a way of getting through this without telling her the truth. At least part of it.

Walker and I exchanged looks, clearly on the same page, but it was Bishop who pulled the trigger. I hadn't even heard the man join us until his voice cut through the silence.

"River's been taken."

"Taken? Like the Liam Neeson movie?"

Bishop nodded.

"So what's this for?"

"Ransom," he said smoothly.

"Oh God," she whimpered. "Has anyone told Bear? He'll want to help. He still knows some guys from his days in the service. He can call in favors. He—"

She was talking fast, clearly in the midst of a panic spiral.

Bishop cut off her ramble, his words blunt but gentle despite that. "Bear's dead. He died trying to keep her from being taken."

Well, that was one way to tell her. I was all for ripping off the Band-aid, but this seemed a bit extreme. Especially in the wake of the River bomb he'd just lobbed at her.

"Wh-what?"

Her knees gave out, McCreedy catching her before she could hit the ground. The bag she'd been clutching didn't fare as well. It fell to the ground with a heavy thud.

"Jonah . . . I can't . . . it can't be true," she whispered, the words turning to sobs.

As Jackson comforted the shattered woman in his arms, Bishop calmly strolled to the bag and picked it up, ignoring the scene he'd caused.

Returning to us, he said quietly, "My intel says she'll be the final lot of the night."

I gritted my teeth, hating that these fuckers were going to parade her around like my wife was theirs to possess.

Gigi cast a tearful but suspicious gaze our way, proving once again that she was every inch her brother's sister. "Intel? Why does a ranch hand have intel about River? What else are you guys hiding?"

"Uh . . ." Walker started, casting a worried glance between us and the crying woman.

Just because we knew Bishop's truth didn't mean we could hand it out freely. But at this point, we just needed to be done with this conversation. We didn't have time for a long, drawn-out story.

Bishop looked to me, then back at Gigi. "I'm not exactly a ranch hand."

"He's FBI," I offered, trying not to make it a big fucking deal. "And it's probably best you don't ask any more questions."

McCreedy was fuming. I could understand it. As our lawyer, it was his job to keep our asses out of jail. Fraternizing with an FBI agent was basically in direct opposition to his key directive. And now there was one more witness he'd have to deal with.

"Just don't come crawling to me when you get yourselves dead," he grumbled.

"Isn't that pretty much impossible?" Walker asked in a poor excuse of a whisper.

McCreedy ignored my brother. Instead, tucking Gigi into his side, he made to put her back in the car. "Now I've gotta deal with this. Fuck, I hate it when women cry."

Instead of allowing herself to be herded, Gigi locked her legs and stood her ground. "I'm staying here."

"Was she invited?" Walker asked.

"I want to be here when River gets back. And this was the last place my brother was alive. I'll feel closer to them both here than in some frou-frou hotel room."

Honestly, I understood her better than I thought I would. I'd want the same thing. She was River's family. Plus, now that she knew the truth, there was no reason to send her away. I was willing to bet Virginia Blake would chew off her own leg before doing anything to put River at risk.

"She stays. Jackson, set her up in the first-floor guest suite." Turning to Gigi, I softened my voice and explained, "That's where your brother was staying. All his things are still there."

With a curt nod of her wobbly chin, she shrugged out of Jackson's hold and made her way into the house.

"You should stay too, Jackson. Until this all blows over, no one is safe," Walker said.

"Y'all don't pay me enough for this shit," he said with a beleaguered sigh.

Once they were inside, I turned my attention back to Bishop. "Was it really the best move letting her in on your secret?"

"Technically, you're the one who shared it."

"Oh, right. Sorry."

He shrugged. "I don't fucking care anymore. I'll answer to the feds later. Right now, I just want to get her back."

"Then let's get ready. We've got two hours to go until she's home where she belongs."

eleven

• • •

River

"Is the blindfold really necessary? I have no fucking clue where we are whether I can see or not." Internally I winced at the high-pitched whine. Honestly, I was just doing my damnedest to annoy Pytor as he sat resolutely beside me in the back of whatever vehicle we were in. "You're gonna mess up my makeup."

"Shut up."

"You should have gagged me."

"That can be arranged."

Something about his darkly amused tone gave me the impression he wasn't planning on using a regular ol' piece of cloth. Thank God I couldn't tell whether he was sporting a boner. That would send my hard-fought bravado back to Neverland.

"Careful, I bite."

"Of course you do. Whoever buys you will have his work cut out for him."

A shiver of apprehension slithered down my spine. I hadn't allowed myself to consider the possibility of *after*. To be fair, I hadn't exactly considered my reality much at all outside of my immediate situation. The thought of being bought and sold, being owned by a stranger, made me want to vomit. I couldn't even let my mind go there.

Denial, you might be a River after all.

I couldn't breathe.

The car slowed and made a right turn before coming to an unexpected stop.

Oh God. Were we here already?

No. I wasn't ready.

A cold, tingling sensation washed over me as my heart rate spiked. Fear? Anxiety? All of the above? Maybe I'd hyperventilate and lose consciousness before they could trot me out for the buyers.

An involuntary tremor worked its way through my muscles, and my gut twisted into a knot.

His hand clamped around my wrist at the same time I heard a door open, and the warm breeze of a southern night hit me. Frogs and crickets were my only soundtrack as he tugged me hard until I stood on wobbly feet, the crunch of gravel under the soles of my stilettos urging me to tread carefully.

"Hurry up," my captor grunted.

"I'm going to break my ankle. I can't see, and the ground is uneven. Where did you bring me? The stockyards?"

He didn't even bother answering that one. He simply tightened his hold on me and practically dragged me behind him.

"You know, for a guy who got real pissy about me being marked up, you are doing a *terrible* job preventing that very thing right now. I don't think road rash is going to be a big selling point. People don't much like pus and oozing wounds."

"You'd be surprised what gets people off."

I blanched. I think that was supposed to be his version of a joke. He wasn't funny.

"Walk forward."

"No."

"Walk, or I'll throw you over my shoulder and give everyone an early preview of what they're buying on our way inside."

"That's not much of an incentive, Sergi. What's a couple of hours in the grand scheme of things? They're going to see it all eventually, right?"

"That's not my name."

"Ask me if I care."

Somehow my fire had been reignited. Maybe it was the imminent auction or the fact I'd been held captive and forced to live in a drugged stupor for who knew how long, but I was spoiling for a fight. And if I was staring down the end of the barrel, I might as well go out swinging. Or whatever the expression was.

I wasn't a meek creature by nature. I blame the drugs and disorientation for the state I'd been reduced to while locked in my cell. But out here, with the wind brushing across my skin and smelling of home, I felt like myself again. Like if I could just break free and run for it, I might be able to make it back to the arms of my men.

Pytor shoved me from behind, hard enough I stumbled forward. He didn't try to catch me, but I also kept my balance—barely. "Walk forward, bitch."

I'd kill him first.

Definitely.

But I took a begrudging step, then another, and another, until I reached a paved area and the cocksucking dickstain pushing me finally stopped.

The air changed too, somehow growing both oppressive and thick with anticipation. It was hard to explain the reason for the change with my eyes covered, but it sort of felt like walking into a cool supermarket after being outside in the hot sun. Except instead of a supermarket, it was a meat market, and I was the piece of ass for sale.

The sweat on my skin instantly chilled, and the air no longer smelled like a familiar combination of dirt and sweet grass. It was replaced by the artificial scent of roses, citrus, and jasmine. And maybe a hint of Aqua Net. It was cloying and reminded me of being backstage the one time I was in a beauty pageant.

The blindfold was removed, and I was shoved into a chair, Pytor glowering down at me.

"Stay. Someone will come for you when it's your turn."

He left, slamming the door behind him, and I finally turned around to take in my new jail cell. I wasn't alone this time. A handful of women—if you could call some of them that—sat huddled around the space. All wearing similarly revealing slip dresses, all made up just like me, all terrified. A few of them looked young enough to be in high school.

Christ, we were one rhinestone choker away from being a group of high-class escorts waiting for our johns to drop by for a visit. Or, given the age of some of these girls, maybe it was more like a sorority.

I was going to be sick.

From the looks of things, I wasn't the only one. A couple of us braver souls made eye contact with one another while others wept silently. Any time someone tried to talk, they were stopped with a look from the older woman in the corner. She wasn't for sale. That much was clear, but she was definitely afraid of the Russians.

Time marched on, one girl after another being removed from the room and not returning. Until the only one left was me.

"Why are you helping them?" I asked the woman in the corner, unable to keep the accusation from my tone.

She simply shook her head and cast her eyes down.

They may not have her up for sale, but she was theirs.

Precious seconds were slipping away. If I was going to make a run for it, she was my only hope. I opened my mouth, intent on trying to convince her that if we worked together, we could make it. But then the door opened again.

Time's up.

My heart fell to my feet. There was no avoiding what was coming. No amount of denial was going to change my fate.

I was going to be sold.

I shouldn't have come back to Devil's Grove when Senior summoned me. I should've let Twisted Cross Ranch rot. But a pang of utter loss hit me hard at the same time those thoughts sent me reeling. If I hadn't come back, I wouldn't have them. Would it have been different if I'd just accepted everything and let Cross love me? I'd been stubborn and hurt, unwilling to admit he still meant something to me. And now I'd never see Cross, Walker, or Sterling again.

How was this the end of my story? How did I even end up here?

There was no way this was really happening. That this was actually my life. It all felt like one tragic dream I couldn't wake up from.

"No, please," I whimpered, unable to stop the pleas from falling from my lips.

There was no brazening my way out. No pretending this wasn't happening.

I was fucking terrified, and I couldn't hide it.

Pytor offered me a grin that looked purely sinister. "I like it when you beg and cry. So will they. Keep it up."

He wrapped his palm around the nape of my neck, the place Sterling always touched me. It sent chills down my spine now, and not the good kind. I shuddered, nausea coiling in a reflexive response to this man's touch.

"Get your fucking hands off me. I can walk on my own."

A dark chuckle escaped him. "You certainly can."

He didn't release me.

Motherfucker.

"So help me God, if you don't release me right now, I'm going to stab you to death with my stiletto."

He laughed, the low rumble reminding me of thunder preceding a deadly storm. "Oh, malyshka, you could try."

As we approached the deep red velvet curtain separating this hallway from what I assumed was the den of sick, twisted men who would attend something like this, my heart hammered.

I hadn't known what to expect, given the storeroom we'd been locked in. I'd sort of guessed it was a restaurant of some kind, maybe a club. But no, this was so much worse. Not because it was some depraved dungeon or anything, but because it was so fucking normal. Sins like this should not be allowed in a living room that could double as a museum. Or perhaps a library.

The scent of wood polish mingled with tobacco and brandy. Floor-to-ceiling woodwork, carved with intricate designs, framed dark green papered walls. Taxidermy animals posed in eerily lifelike ways were scattered around, giving this house the feel of a macabre hunting lodge. The haze of cigar smoke hung over the heads of the masked men seated in velvet club chairs as they talked and laughed together like they weren't fucking disgusting pigs.

They broke out into hushed murmurs as I was escorted into the room. I could feel their eyes on me like a series of unwanted caresses as they sized me up. One man blatantly adjusted himself as they rushed me past. I forced myself to look away before I did something brave but stupid. Like bum-rush him and rip his dick off before beating him with it.

Where were the other women? Had they already been purchased? Guilt and grief overtook me and nearly brought me to my knees. I'd done nothing to help them. But what could I have hoped to achieve? I was unarmed, outnumbered, and sadly, outmuscled.

"Get on the stage, malyshka. Undress. Don't make me do it for you."

Gritting my teeth, I took the stairs slowly, unable to bring my gaze to meet the eyes of any of my potential new owners.

"And now, the one you've all been waiting for. Our prize. Lot 723. Age twenty-eight. While not a virgin, this one has never given birth, but bloodwork shows she's healthy and fertile. She's fiery, with a will I know you're all eager to break."

My kidnapper gestured for me to remove my dress. I didn't. I may not have control over much, but I still had that. Perhaps my resistance was futile, but when autonomy is all you have, you cling to it. His eyes flashed with malice as he pulled out a pocketknife and stalked forward. I swallowed the bile rising in my throat as Pytor sliced my dress down the front with a growl, letting the fabric flutter to the floor.

They were really auctioning me off like I was breeding stock. Like a heifer at the stockyards. Though I'd rather they kill me than breed me.

A hum of approval went through the crowd as my body was bared for them, and I wanted to slit each of their throats and watch them choke on their own blood. I hated each and every one of these men.

I held my chin high, refusing to cower, even though I was shaking like a leaf on the inside. Let them look. They might *purchase* me, but I would never belong to them. The only men I belonged to were the ones I chose. The ones I willingly gave my heart to.

I cast my gaze around the room, silently cursing each and every asshole I made eye contact with.

Fuck you, Gramps.

Burn in hell, Satan.

My eyes locked onto a pair of midnight blues I would have sworn I recognized. Electricity shot through me, lighting me up as I stared. It was impossible to make out the man's features beneath the mask that concealed everything but his jawline and lips.

My heart leapt, foolishly believing it was Cross. But I killed the hope before it could take root.

No one was coming to rescue me. They would've found me by now.

They were probably all dead.

Just like Bear.

"We'll begin the bidding at—"

"$100,000!" came from the back of the room.

"$125!" This from a man right in front of me, his beady eyes and ruddy cheeks making me take a step backward.

The bidding war went on and on, with nothing from the blue-eyed man who'd seen into my soul earlier. That bitch hope just didn't know when to leave me the fuck alone.

When it finally slowed, we were at a whopping four hundred grand. I didn't know the going rate for a woman, but that seemed like a lot to me. At least it did until I remembered it was *me* they were bidding on. I wasn't sure there was a number high enough that could make what was happening to me palatable, let alone worth it.

"Half a million!" When Blue Eyes spoke, the world dropped out from under me. I may have doubted myself once, but I'd recognize his voice anywhere.

Cross.

He *was* here for me.

I had to work to keep my composure. I couldn't let them see my renewed vigor. They had to think I was still a shell of myself.

Beady Eyes huffed and shouted, "$750!"

Cross stood, calm, casual, and much more together than I expected, eyes locked on mine. "One million."

twelve

• • •

Cross

One hour earlier

"Let's go over this again," I said as Walker drove us down the deserted road, nothing but our headlights cutting through the night.

"What's there to go over? I drive, then Bishop and I sit in the car with our thumbs up our asses while you pay this fucker for your wife."

Bishop shook his head. "I'll be in your ear the whole time, Cross. Just remember, as much as you want to, don't bid until it slows down. She'll know it's you the moment you open your mouth."

"I know how to work a damn auction, thanks."

"Not one like this."

Walker slowed as we approached the crest of a hill, then let out a low whistle. "I think we found it, boys."

The mansion was located on a remote piece of land about an hour out of town. I knew for a fact it wasn't one of Volkov's properties, which meant he'd conned—or more likely blackmailed—someone into using it for the night's festivities. The place screamed opulence. There was a massive fountain in the driveway, with a whole-ass valet stand waiting to receive cars as they pulled in.

"Uh . . . no one planned for valet?" Walker asked, panic in his voice.

"Just say you're the driver. Drop Cross off. Go park. It'll be fine."

Walker pulled his hat down lower to hide his face as we approached the circular driveway. The fountain was lit up like we were attending a party, not an underground auction.

As soon as he stopped, Bishop got out and made a show of opening my door. I adjusted my bowtie, hating that, on top of everything else, I had to wear a goddamn monkey suit. With an aggrieved sigh, I put on my mask before stepping out of the car.

A valet leaned his head into the window, but Walker waved him off. "Just droppin' the boss off. No need for your help. Just point us toward the parking lot where we can wait."

The guy gave him some directions, then approached me, face expectant. I already had a fifty in my palm, ready to bribe him for his cooperation, so I shook his hand and murmured, "Thank you for your discretion. I don't let strangers drive my car. Ever."

"No problem, sir," the guy said, pocketing the cash and heading for the next car in the line.

Bishop's voice crackled in my ear. "No matter what you see, keep your shit together. You're only here for one thing. Walk in like you belong, grab a drink, and take a seat. Don't talk to anyone. Just keep to yourself until it's time. She'll be the last one up."

I didn't bother responding. It was never a good look to be caught talking to yourself.

Large French doors opened into a grand foyer, complete with a spiral staircase and a chandelier I swore I saw in a documentary about Versailles. Men were milling about, no one in any particular hurry to get to the main event.

I guess to them, the women were interchangeable so long as they were the one to break them. Bastards.

It took everything in me not to start tearing motherfuckers apart here and now. It was a good thing they were wearing masks, or I'd have made a note of every fucking one of them and added them to my kill list. Right under Dominik motherfucking Volkov.

"Drink, sir?" a cocktail waitress asked. I'd been so focused on assessing my enemies I hadn't seen her. She blended in somehow in her black skirt and white top. Perhaps it was more that she faded into the background.

"Whiskey, two fingers, neat."

"Right away."

She scurried off, and I wondered how safe it was for her to be here in a place like this. Was she at risk of being taken? Probably. But as far as the outward appearance of this gathering, it was just a regular party filled with the usual rich assholes. If she had any idea about the type of men she was serving, I doubted she would have shown up to work tonight. Women didn't survive in this world without learning how to handle themselves against the unwanted advances of drunk men. Just like bunnies knew to fear and recognize foxes. But neither would have a fucking clue what to do against a T-Rex. And tonight, this poor woman was surrounded by dinosaurs.

I moved through the crowd as soon as the waitress brought me my drink, pretending to sip here and there as I familiarized myself with the exits.

A man dressed in all black with his face fully hidden called out from a set of double doors at the end of the hall. "Gentlemen, please take your seats. The presentation is about to begin."

I joined the other guests, blood humming with apprehension as we made our way into the room where I'd get my sparrow back. One by one, men started taking seats at various low-slung sofas and club chairs set around the parlor. I selected one near the back that gave me a good view of the rest of the space without placing me in anyone's direct line of sight. It also made me the least vulnerable to any kind of attack from behind. Knowing Volkov, he'd clocked me the second I walked through the doors.

Cigars were lit, and the slimy pieces of shit here ready to bid on women happily chatted like it was a normal Saturday night. Until the lights dimmed and the auctioneer stepped up to the podium.

"Welcome, gentlemen. We have a particularly luscious selection for you this evening. Most of you are repeat guests, but in the interest of the few of you who are new to us, bidding works the same as any auction. High bid wins, cash only, payable before prize collection. Don't bid if you can't pay."

He adjusted his paperwork and cleared his throat. "No touching the goods until ownership is transferred. No photography or videography of any kind. Anyone caught with a cell phone will be permanently removed.

"Now that we're clear on the rules, let's begin. Bring out lot 711."

The room was dead silent until a door on the far end opened and a blond man and slender redhead—barely legal if my eyes weren't deceiving me—walked in. I recognized the man immediately, anger causing my blood to boil in my veins. It was the fucker who took River. I had to curl my fingers into the leather of my chair to keep myself from jumping him here and now.

She was paraded into the space like a showhorse, but the poor woman was trembling, tears trailing down her freckled cheeks with each step. Then they made her undress, and I thought I might vomit. I wasn't sure I could do this, and I definitely knew I wouldn't survive seeing River in the same state.

Bids came in hard and fast. The woman ultimately sold to a man who had to be old enough to be her grandfather.

Lifting my drink to cover my moving lips, I asked in a voice barely above a whisper, "How many more?"

"Intel says it's at least a dozen."

Fuck.

There was no way I was going to make it until River's turn.

One after another, they came in, were demoralized, and then sold. And I couldn't do a damn thing to stop it. Then the auctioneer announced a short break while they 'prepared' the final lot for the night. My wife.

"We need to stop this from happening again," I murmured, using the same trick to hide my words.

"People have been trying for years," Bishop said back, somber as ever. "Bastards like this pop up all the time."

Walker's voice filtered into my ear. "Good thing we're richer than

God. I'll donate to every cause there is. Hunt down and kill every asshole who ever participated in the flesh trade. This is fucking sick, and I can't even see it."

"You're not wrong," I muttered.

The door opened again, and my heart damn near stopped.

River.

She barely looked like herself, but my body responded to the sight of her all the same, and I hated myself for it in that moment. Now wasn't the time to think of anything other than saving her. Love made you sloppy. It clouded your judgment. I needed to be sharp for this. I could love on her when she was in my arms, tell her how much she meant to me, and make sure she knew how cherished she was.

"And now, the one you've all been waiting for. Our prize. Lot 723. Age twenty-eight. While not a virgin, this one has never given birth, but bloodwork shows she's healthy and fertile. She's fiery, with a will I know you're all eager to break."

I had to grit my teeth as they shoved her onto the platform and her kidnapper cut the dress off her. It was impossible not to miss the way she curled in on herself, and my gaze zeroed in on the faint bruising on her sides.

They'd pay for that.

Before I left tonight, I'd see about burning this entire place to the ground.

Fuck these assholes. No one deserved to be treated like this.

Her eyes raked across the room, my sparrow making her own kill list if I knew her like I thought I did. But when they landed on me, I saw the jolt of recognition, the little spark of hope.

I sent her a silent, *"It's me, baby. I'm here. It's gonna be fine,"* before she shook off the connection.

The auctioneer tried to start the bidding but was cut off immediately. The men in the room were salivating at the chance to get their hands on my wife. Especially the ones who already lost out to earlier auctions. She was their last chance, and the desperation showed as bidding quickly surpassed the highest ones of the evening. I forced myself to stay silent even though I was itching to bolt up there and take her home. Twice now I'd had to stop myself from removing my coat and rushing to her side.

"Not yet," Bishop said. "Wait for my signal."

I let out a growl of frustration. I wanted her to know I was here for her, that I'd come to bring her back where she was safe.

"Four hundred thousand!"

"Now," Bishop said.

The words flew out of my mouth faster than a bull at a rodeo.

"Half a million!"

I didn't miss the way she tensed at the sound of my voice. She knew for certain now. I'd come for her.

A paunchy man near the front huffed and shouted, "$750!"

I stood, ready to put this to bed. No one would have her but me. Not even over my dead body. I'd kill her myself before letting her suffer that fate.

"One million."

"That'll shut them down. Go claim our girl," Walker said.

I waited for my victory to be announced, for the man to bang his gavel and my prize to be won. Instead I froze in place as Dominik Volkov's voice rang out from the darkened balcony in the back of the parlor.

"Two million dollars. We're done here. Send her to my room."

River gasped, her shocked, "No," hitting me like a knife through the ribs.

The auctioneer looked to me and a desperate agony spread through my chest, settling as a deep pit in my stomach. I didn't have anything else. I was fucking tapped out.

Volkov looked down at me, his knowing smirk and cold icy irises revealing what I'd already suspected. He'd been lying in wait all this time. The sonofabitch wasn't even wearing a mask. He wanted me to know I'd been outplayed.

But if that sick bastard thought I was going to back down, he was about to learn a serious lesson. One he'd take with him to the grave. Because that's where he was going.

Spinning around, I stormed out of the room.

Not giving a damn who heard, I said, "It's time for Plan B."

thirteen

. . .

River

"Get inside," Pytor snarled as he shoved me through yet another door and into yet another room.

This time it wasn't a dank cell. But the large four-poster bed with handcuffs attached to a bar on the headboard had me wishing for my disgusting nest. At least there, I knew I'd be left alone.

Nothing good was going to happen to me in this room.

In this bed.

I'd already been sold, and Alexei had proven assault wasn't off the table, so was rape really much of a stretch?

Seeing Cross in the crowd had filled me with renewed spirit. He was here, which meant Walker and Bishop wouldn't be far off. They'd come for me. I just had to stay alive long enough for them to get here.

"You know, the more I get to know you, Mikhail, the more I realize what a little bitch you are."

Pytor made a low growling sound. In another life, it would've scared the snot out of me. Hell, even an hour ago, it would've worked. Not anymore. That was before I had hope again.

"Stop your incessant yapping. Like a fucking bitch dog." He dragged me by my arms toward the bed.

"I don't know. It seems to me like you're the bitch in this situation."

That one brought him up short. "How do you figure?"

"Well, I mean, you were the one in charge of feeding me, grooming me, cleaning my cage, picking up my shit. I feel like I got the better end of the deal. I only had to deal with seeing your ugly face a couple of times a week. So tell me, Kyrill, who's the real bitch here? Me, or you?"

"Shut the fuck up."

"Never gonna happen. You're stuck with me. Bitch." I purposely drew it out, making the word as long as I possibly could.

I knew it was working when his cheeks turned a mottled crimson. He drew his arm back like he was going to backhand me, and damn it all, I flinched.

Missing nothing, he checked the movement and chuckled menacingly, staring me down. "Pretty soon you'll be Volkov's problem. Since I'm feeling generous, I'll let you choose. On your back, or on your belly?"

"Don't you think he'll kill you for taking what he bought?"

God, I hoped he was bluffing.

He shoved me onto the bed and began working at his belt. Shit, he wasn't bluffing. "It'll be worth the pain if I get to make you cry as I fill you with my cum."

I made a show of gagging, using the moment to clock the knife tucked in a sheath attached to his leather belt. I wasn't sure whether it was the same one he'd used on my dress earlier, but honestly, it didn't matter. A knife was a knife. If I could get my hands on it, I'd make it fucking count.

I'd use a damn nail file to stab him in the eye right now if it was all I had.

Weapons were what you made of them, after all. Wasn't that a saying? It should be. I had a feeling anything could be deadly with the right inspiration.

"If you can even get it up. I doubt I'd even feel a thing. Your pencil dick isn't enough for me."

He fondled his knife. "Who said anything about using my dick?"

My bravado faltered for several heartbeats until I remembered he couldn't do anything that would leave visible marks. Not with

Volkov on his way. He wouldn't risk his boss's wrath. This was all posturing.

I hoped.

Just to be safe, though, I definitely needed to get my hands on that weapon.

"Maybe I will use my cock first. Since you mentioned it."

Bile burned in the back of my throat, but I forced myself to roll my eyes. "So fucking predictable, Igor. Way to be a walking stereotype."

Inside, I was screaming. But as the words left my lips, I felt like a badass bitch. Fake it till you make it, right?

He shoved his pants down enough to expose his pathetic, floppy cock, only at half-mast even now.

I let out a snort. "Is that all there is? God, I probably have a better chance of busting a hymen with my fingers than you do with that inchworm."

"According to your past, your hymen was long gone. How many of them did you take at once? All three? Dirty fucking whore."

"Aw, what's wrong? Are you jealous?"

He gripped me around the throat and shoved me hard onto my back, cutting off my air supply as he forced his hips between my legs. Instead of panicked clawing at his hand, I reached down, fumbling until I grabbed the switchblade and freed it from the sheath. He must've realized what I was doing because he tensed and made to move, but I was too fast. I opened the knife and plunged it deep into his side. The blade slid cleanly between his ribs, making him gasp and pull back. I yanked the knife free and didn't waste a fucking second, even as blood slid down his torso and began dripping onto me. I brought the knife down as hard and fast as I could, hitting him at the juncture of his thigh and pelvis. A kill shot Bear had taught me.

"When in doubt, always aim for an artery, cub. You don't have to be super precise or deal with cutting around bone, and just a nick will get the job done."

Pytor's eyes went wide as blood sprayed over me, pulse after pulse matching the beat of his heart.

He opened his mouth, bright red bubbles dribbling down his chin.

"What was that? I didn't quite make it out," I taunted, clinging to this violent savagery I'd somehow unleashed. I was sure shock would claim me soon, but before it did, I intended to ride this wave as long as possible.

When all he managed was a slow blink, I gave him my best go fuck yourself smile and used my leg to kick him off the bed. He fell with a heavy thud, and I winced, eyes darting to the door, sure he had backup waiting to rush in.

I got onto my knees in the center of the bed, knife poised and ready to strike. They'd kill me, but I'd go down fighting like hell.

After all, my Bear raised me right.

It could have been seconds or hours later; I had absolutely zero concept of time as I waited. Finally a scratch came at the door, followed by the turn of the knob.

My heart raced.

My palms sweat.

But through it all, I forced myself to hold steady, my gaze never leaving the door.

Whoever this was better make themselves right with their God, because I was about to take them to meet him.

I wasn't sure who was more shocked when it finally opened.

Me.

Or Bishop.

Bishop

WIND BLEW in from the open window I'd just climbed through. I had ten minutes tops to find her and get us both out. Thank God Asher came through with the blueprints of this place. Otherwise I'd never get to her in time.

Volkov and his crew were occupied with closing out the auction, which meant for a short time, she'd be alone. Or at least not heavily guarded. One Russian asshole I could deal with. An army? Not without backup.

Slow and even breaths kept me focused as I crept down the hall, my eyes trained on the nearest door. I had no idea which room she'd be in, but I'd try every single one until I found her. Heart pounding, I reached for the first knob with my free hand, my gun pointed at chest level. I swung it open slowly, the lack of lights telling me this wasn't the one. Still, years of training dictated I clear the room before moving on.

I made a point to shut the door behind me as I moved on, not wanting to leave accidental breadcrumbs and tip Volkov or his boys off to the fact that I'd been here. I was just getting ready to see what was behind door number two when muffled voices hit my ears. Everything in me went cold and tight, and I immediately ditched the door I was at and took off at a careful run, following the voices until the unmistakable sounds of a scuffle came from just beyond the final bedroom in this corridor.

Thank fuck I'd heard them, or I'd have spent all my time checking empty rooms.

You don't know this is her. One of the other girls could have been brought up here.

I shook off the thought. If it wasn't her, then I'd save this one and send the prick who purchased her straight to hell.

No one deserved this fate.

Even amped up as I was, my movements were controlled, my thoughts clear. It had been far easier than I'd imagined to slip back into this role. My body knew exactly what it needed to do to get the job done.

I tightened my grip on the butt of my gun with one hand while slowly twisting the knob of the door with my other.

I'd only just cracked it open when the metallic tang of blood hit my nose.

No. Fuck, not again. Not her too.

I shoved the door open, took one look at the crimson chaos of the room, and fucking snapped.

I was too fucking late.

Again.

But then I blinked and realized it wasn't too late.

My siren was there, on her knees, soaked in blood, with a knife held out in one shaking hand. She locked eyes with me and gasped before dropping the weapon and falling forward, collapsing on the bed, hurt but alive.

"Sterling?"

Her voice shook almost as badly as her body.

I ran toward her, desperate to stanch the flow of blood. "Where are you hurt?"

"It's not mine." Her words didn't register as I started checking for injuries. "Sterling, it's not mine."

My eyes snapped back to hers. I repeated her words, my brain struggling to believe them. "It's not your blood."

She shook her head, reaching for me and catching herself at the last second, bloodied hands hovering inches from my face.

I grabbed her by the nape and pulled her against me, kissing her for all I was worth. Everything I'd ever wanted was right here in my arms, and I'd be damned if anyone would take her from me.

Pulling back, she jutted her chin to the side of the bed and whispered, "It's his. I k-killed him."

I risked a glance away from her for the barest second as I took in the body on the floor. His eyes were open but sightless, mouth slack with a crimson trail falling from the corner. His jeans were open, his blood-covered cock on display.

"Did he . . . fuck, did he . . ." I couldn't bring myself to say the word.

"No," she rasped, then repeated more forcefully. "No. I stopped him before he could."

I could have sunk to the floor, such was my relief. Thank fuck.

"That's my girl. Are you sure he didn't hurt you?"

"I'm okay, Sterling. I just want to go home."

All too aware of the seconds slipping by, I shrugged off my shirt and handed it to her. "Then let's go home."

"How are we going to get out of here? They'll see us. We can't just walk out the front door."

I tugged her toward the exit. "Did you forget? I'm a super spy. We're going out the window."

She let out a startled huff of laughter. "You might be a super spy, but I wasn't trained to scale walls with my bare hands."

"Guess you'll just have to trust me."

Her eyes held mine, and without an ounce of hesitation, she murmured, "I do."

She didn't know what those words meant to me. How her easy acceptance and willingness to place her life in my hands even after the hell she'd just been through was the equivalent of her giving me the whole fucking world.

I vowed then and there to spend the rest of my days proving to her that I was worth it. Worthy of the love and trust she gave me so effortlessly. I would never let her down again.

fourteen

• • •

Walker

"Where are they? They should've been out here by now."
My gut churned with every passing second as Cross and I waited in the car, lights off, engine idling, attention focused on the window Bishop slipped through nearly fifteen minutes ago. The plan had been ten. Max.

I was certain men would come swarming out of the mansion any second, weapons trained on us.

"I'm not cut out for this," I muttered, my knee bouncing and fingers tapping on the steering wheel.

"He'll get her out."

"And what if he doesn't?"

"Then we go in after them."

I scoffed. "That's a suicide mission."

Burning midnight blues hit mine. "Are you saying she's not worth dying for?"

"Don't put words in my mouth."

"Then stop your fucking whining."

I lifted my gaze back to the window, staring so hard the image blurred, and I had to blink. My heart lurched as a shadow passed in front of the curtain. Then a large figure ducked out and climbed onto the trellis. Fuck. He had her. She was clinging to his back like a koala.

"Is that blood?" Cross snarled. "If she's hurt . . ."

"She's alive. Let's save the vengeance for after we have her safe."

Cross grunted, already climbing out of the car and rushing around to help them get in.

"It's not hers," Bishop said without preamble, carefully untangling River's arms from around his neck. Sweat dotted his brow and lines bracketed his mouth. I'd bet Blue's life the tension radiating from him had nothing to do with exertion and everything to do with the prolonged physical contact. Even in a rescue situation, it had to be playing hell on his PTSD. He'd shared a bit of his past with me when he'd stopped by after my attack to offer some advice on dealing with my burns. Turned out we had more in common than our obsession with River.

"Give her to me," Cross said. "It's okay."

Bishop passed our girl to Cross, then heaved a sigh, his body visibly relaxing. We'd done it. We had her with us. It was almost over. But a shout echoed from the house, setting us all on high alert.

"Get in the fucking car," I growled. "We've gotta move."

Keeping River cradled on his lap, Cross settled them in the back seat while Bishop took the place next to me, gun aimed and ready as I peeled out.

"Go, go, go!" Bishop shouted, rolling down the window and firing two shots as men raced from the house.

They might have had guns, but I drove like a bat out of hell. I floored it, leaving them in a cloud of dust as we sped off.

"We're never going to be safe," River said, her voice a harsh, fearful rasp. "He'll come for me. He won't ever stop."

"Shh, baby. I promise you we will. You're safe now. We're going to do everything to keep you protected." The way my brother's voice was so different from the Cross I'd grown up with shocked me. He soothed her so easily with words and actions. From the rearview mirror, I watched him stroke her hair and kiss the top of her head over and over. "We've got you, sweetness. No one's ever going to hurt you again."

"We can't go back to the ranch, can we?" she asked some time later.

"No, ladybug. It's the first place they'll look."

"So where, then?"

"We found a place to hunker down," Bishop said, his eyes lifting to meet hers in the rearview mirror. "A few hours away. Remote. Secure. I personally checked out the specs. It's basically a fortress."

"Hiding? Is that how this is going to go? Are we just going to spend our lives running from him?"

I glanced out of the corner of my eye in time to see Bishop's expression turn to granite.

"No," he said firmly.

"So what's the plan, then?"

"I'm going to hunt the bastard down and kill him."

"Stand in line," Cross growled, his arms tightening around River. "I called dibs."

Part of me felt like I should throw my hat in the ring, make a declaration of my own. But honestly, I was less worried about getting vengeance and more interested in taking care of my girl. Everyone else had a chance to hold her and make sure she knew they loved her. I was ready for it to be my turn.

THREE HOURS LATER, I was desperate to get out of this fucking car and stretch my aching legs. We were nearly there, though. One last turn up a winding dirt road. Then I'd be able to touch her and see with my own eyes that she was okay.

She'd fallen asleep almost immediately, though it was far from restful. Every now and then, little whimpers would slip free, and she wouldn't settle down until Cross whispered reassurances in her ear.

One thing was abundantly clear: my ladybug had been horribly mistreated. She'd lost weight she could ill afford to lose, and despite the makeup caking her face, it looked as though she'd been knocked around a bit. The blood flaking off her limbs didn't help matters either.

"What's that scowl for?" Bishop asked.

"I'm not scowling."

"Uh huh."

"I'm just trying to decide if she needs a burger or a shower first."

He hummed in consideration. "It's late. She needs sleep."

"Shower," came her soft reply as I keyed in the gate code, then drove through. "I'm not hungry."

"You got it, darlin'," I said, aiming for relaxed and easy but unable to hide the break in my voice.

"Does Ransom have a doc on call?" Cross asked.

"Should do," I confirmed.

"We need someone here to check her over. We all saw the bruise in that photo, and I saw the rest of her body when they made her undress. I didn't like the look of the bruises on her sides."

"They didn't hit me much. Mostly just drugged my food," she murmured sleepily.

My knuckles went white on the wheel. "I hope you flay those fuckers alive," I gritted out.

"I intend to," Bishop swore.

"Not if I get there first," River threatened. She sounded more like a kitten than an alley cat, but I could still appreciate her bloodlust.

I chuckled. "My girl is fierce."

"Don't you forget it."

Parking the car in front of the sprawling lake house, I shut off the engine and got out before opening the door for my brother. "Come on, we're here."

Her eyes swept across the darkened landscape. It was impossible to make out much of anything without the light pollution of the city, but the mansion loomed over us, making no secret of its size.

"Where's here?" she asked.

"Somewhere safe," was all I said. I needed her in my arms in the worst way.

"I called in a favor," Cross added.

"A favor that got you a new house?"

"We're borrowing it. It's not mine. Unless you want it, then I'll see what I can do."

I rolled my eyes at my brother's promise, though my lips twitched with a silent laugh. It was exactly the shit he'd pull. Me too, for that matter. Whatever our girl wanted, we'd get for her. Anything to make her happy. No matter who we had to fuck over or double cross to make it happen.

"Whose house is this, Cross?"

"Brett Ransom."

"Why do I know that name? And why do I hear water?"

I let out a soft laugh. "He's basically the Bruce Wayne of ranchers." When she gave me a curious look, I added, "He's the second richest man in Texas, and this is his private sanctuary. The guy wanted somewhere to get away from everything. So he bought a damn forest and had a lake made, then built a house right on the shore."

"Classy," she murmured, but I could tell her energy was flagging.

"Let's get you inside, pretty girl. See about getting you all cleaned up and tucked in bed."

Grabbing my cane, I held out an arm for her, silently asking her to join me. She did so gratefully, curling into my side and settling some of the restless ache in my chest.

"You two coming?" I asked without looking over my shoulder.

"You go on ahead," Bishop answered. "I want to do a sweep of the perimeter before I come in."

"I'll join you," Cross said, turning to follow him.

As soon as we stepped foot on the porch, light flooded the area, startling us both. The front door swung open, and both Bishop and Cross pulled their guns on instinct. River fisted my shirt, tucking her body against mine. She'd never been one to scare easily, but after the last few weeks, I could tell she wasn't going to take to strangers—especially male ones—anytime soon.

"Whoa, don't shoot. I'm just here to help get you settled." Ransom stood in the doorway, hands up, a twinkle in his eye.

"Fuck, Ransom. We didn't know you'd be here." Cross holstered his weapon and approached the man, hand extended.

Bishop seemed less inclined to relax. He lowered his gun but didn't put it away, even after Cross and Ransom shook hands.

"There's too much y'all don't know about the place to keep from tripping alarms. Besides, we're in this together now."

"No, we're not," I bit out, frustrated he was here without telling us.

"Yeah, we are. I'm not leaving you out in the cold with Volkov on your heels. Cross helped me when I was in a jam once. It's time I return the favor."

"The favor was use of your house, not you playing butler."

"Yeah, well, I come with the house, so suck it up. Now come on, get inside. Looks like y'all have had a rough night and could use a good night's sleep." He eyed River, and I tightened my hold on her. "I'll get a doc up here in the morning after you've had some rest, River."

She nodded and whispered, "Thank you."

Ransom's gaze met mine, a multitude of questions there, but he didn't ask a single one. "Follow me. We'll get you all set up."

"I was gonna do a security sweep," Bishop protested.

"I can do you one better. Let me get your girl sorted out, and then I'll show you my control room."

There was no way I'd leave her for a bunch of computer screens. "I'll stay with her."

"Suit yourself."

Cross looked like he wanted to debate the issue, probably try and squeeze in on my alone time with her, but he shocked me by staying silent. Guess old dogs could learn new tricks.

Ransom led us upstairs to a suite, complete with a view of the lake, the moon shining over the water. The picture would have been beautiful and romantic if we weren't coming off a horrific trauma. He left us alone, pointing out the fresh towels and spare clothes he'd already set out before telling me we could call down to the control room if we needed anything else. We wouldn't. I planned to get my girl cleaned up and safely snuggled in bed where I could make sure she knew she was safe.

"Do you need help in the shower, ladybug?"

She bit down on her lower lip, looking torn. "I'd rather do it myself if that's okay."

I got it. She needed time alone to take stock of herself and reclaim her agency. "You don't have to ask permission, darlin'. I just wanted to make sure you didn't need me."

"I always need you," she murmured so softly I thought I imagined it.

"You want me. There's a difference. And I'm so glad you do. Just holler at me if you decide you want help. I'll be here."

"'Kay. I'll be fast."

"Take all the time you need. I'm not going anywhere."

Something about the way I said it caught her attention, and she paused with her hand on the doorframe, holding my gaze for a beat before she said, "Me either." Then she moved into the bathroom, keeping the door open behind her.

It wasn't an invitation, and I didn't take it as one. After her captivity, it made sense she wasn't going to be a big fan of closed doors for a while. At least not in unfamiliar places.

The realization that we'd all be forever changed because of that slimy bastard Volkov finally caught up with me.

I held it together until the shower started and she stepped into the stall. Then the walls I'd put up came crumbling down, and I lost it. My breaths came in frantic gulps as I sat on the edge of the bed, head in my hands, heart racing. I let myself break down while she cleaned her attacker's blood off her body, and I prayed she wouldn't come out until I pulled it together. Not because I was ashamed, but because the last thing she needed was the burden of my emotional turmoil.

We might never be able to reclaim the pieces of us he'd stolen. Her sense of safety. My ability to walk without a limp. And so many other things the four of us may not discover for years to come.

But at least we were together.

We'd figure out the rest and learn to live with it.

fifteen

• • •

River

It took three rounds of suds to get that disgusting pig's blood off me. I scrubbed until my skin was pink from the friction and didn't come out until the water ran clear, my fingernails were spotless, and I could no longer feel his hot breath on my face.

Turning off the water, I grabbed a plush towel off the rack and wrapped it around my body. Then I paused between the stall and the still-open door. I knew Walker was out there standing guard, but I wasn't quite ready to join him yet. My brain was still a jumble, and I needed just a little bit longer to return to myself fully.

Thinking if I could see with my own eyes that I was okay, that I was here, that this was real, might help ease some of that anxious energy, I wiped my hand over the fogged mirror and stared at the woman in the glass.

Spoiler, it was me.

I wasn't surprised by that, obviously, but if I'm being honest, it sort of felt like after these last few weeks, something would be different. Like there would be some marker on my skin testifying to the horrors I'd endured.

But no. No outward scar. No scarlet letter.

Just me.

River Adams-Cross. (We'd address how fucking weird that hyphen was later)

Long blonde hair, though wet and hanging in my face, eyes a vibrant green, the same rise to my left eyebrow I'd always been annoyed by, and a slightly crooked nose. This was a face I knew so well, though thinner, paler, and more beat up than usual. I looked like myself on the outside but needed to come to terms with who my experiences made me on the inside. No, not *who* they made me. What I *allowed* them to make me.

I chose not to let them change a damn thing about me. I fought tooth and nail to get away. I killed Pytor. I stared into his eyes as his blood left his body. And I'd do it again in a heartbeat.

I was not the victim here.

I was a survivor.

No one could take that from me—not unless I let them.

And I think I'd done more than enough to prove I never would.

I watched as the woman in the mirror adjusted her posture. Between one breath and the next, her shoulders were a little straighter, her chin just a bit higher, the spark in her eyes a hint brighter.

There was even the slightest smile ghosting her lips.

There you are, River.

On the heels of that somewhat silly thought came another.

I missed you.

"Darlin'? You okay in there?" Walker's question had my belly tightening, but not with fear. I'd missed him too. So much.

A flash of the dream I'd had when lost in a drug haze hit me hard. What I'd wanted more than anything else had been my three men. I had them back now, and I wanted to make the most of it.

It was time for me to reclaim everything those motherfuckers had tried to deny me.

Especially my future with the men I loved.

Loosening my towel, I pivoted toward the open door, letting the wet terry cloth drop to the floor.

Walker's eyes went comedically wide. "What . . . uh . . . what are you doing?"

"Surely you know a proposition when you see one, Walker Cross."

"River, no. You've just been to hell and back. I'm not about to—"

"You stop right there, Walker Wayne. Don't you dare look at me like I am some fragile, broken thing. This is my body. My *choice*. You don't get to make it for me. Now if you don't want me, if *you* are the one who needs more time, that's different. But don't say no because you think you're protecting me. Don't change my story by turning me into someone who needs to be pitied. I survived. I am right fucking here, and I want to wash away the memory of what they did with your touch. Now are you going to help me, or do I need to—"

"C'mere, River. Let me show you exactly how much I want you. I'm never going to deny you a damn thing you ask for. Not in this life or the next."

He pushed to his feet, and I could tell that while the weeks had done a lot for his recovery, he still wasn't quite one hundred percent. Knowing his pride would force him to prove otherwise if I mentioned it, I went to him and gently but forcefully shoved him back to the bed. Straddling his hips, I wrapped my arms around his neck and leaned in to bring our lips together.

He groaned the moment our mouths collided, his tongue pressing inside, the hunger in his kiss sending a curl of need straight to my clit.

"That's more like it."

He grinned at me. "You gonna take me for a ride, baby?"

"Yes, please."

Finally I was able to think about myself without the ghost of what they did to me in the foreground. This was just me and Walker, right here, in the moment. No Russian mob, no horrible people doing horrible things.

"I've missed you so much," Walker said, his voice rough with desire.

"Take off your clothes, Walker. I'm right here. You don't have to miss me anymore."

His lips quirked up in his signature sexy smirk. "That's a little hard to do with you sitting on me, darlin'."

I raised a brow. "Since when are you a quitter?"

"Who said anything about quittin'? A smart man knows when to ask for help, is all."

"That so?" I asked, reaching between us as I worked on undoing his belt.

His eyes darkened. "I'm pretty sure someone somewhere said it once upon a time. Can't quite recall the specifics when your—"

The rest of his words were lost to a groan as I wrapped my hand around his hard length.

"What was that you were saying?"

"Fuck if I know."

I ripped open his shirt, thankful as hell for the snaps on western wear because his chest was bared to me in seconds, all that warm, tattooed skin at my disposal. I wanted to wrap myself up in him and never leave. I wanted him to imprint himself on my body so thoroughly that even if we were apart, I'd never forget what he felt like moving inside me.

"God, you're so beautiful," I murmured, trailing my fingers across his hard chest, down to the stacked muscles across his abdomen, until I found the pierced crown of his cock again. "Look at you, dripping for me."

"Jesus, you're killing me with this dominant talk. I think I might have a praise kink."

"And here I thought you were a big bad alpha male."

"Darlin', I'll be whatever you want me to be."

I smiled as his words and their meaning washed over me. I realized then that *this* was exactly what I needed. That it had to be Walker. Sterling or Cross would want to be in charge; they were too dominant to cede their control. But right now, I was reclaiming *my* control. Walker was the only one of my men who could help give that back to me. And I loved him for it.

"Fuck, your pussy is so hot and slick. I can feel it all over my dick, baby."

I rolled my hips, grinding down onto him and sending little bolts of electricity through both of us. When his piercing hit my clit, I moaned. "Christ, I forgot about that thing."

"My dick? Baby, you're hurting my feelings."

"Your piercing," I gasped when his hands dug into my ass and pressed me more firmly against that magic bit of metal.

"Listen, I'm all for you being controlling in the bedroom"—he rocked his hips and brushed against me again, groaning as my cunt clenched along his shaft—"ungh, God, do that again. But if you don't either sit on my cock or sit on my face in the next ten seconds, I'm gonna take over and fuck you into next week."

"You say that like it's a bad thing."

He chuckled, but it was a strained rasp. "It will be when Cross comes looking for us. You know how jealous he gets. He'll probably do something macho and possessive, like fuck you in the ass while I'm still buried in your sweet little pussy."

"Je-sus, Walker."

"What'd I say?"

"You know what you did." I lifted onto my knees, then positioned him at my entrance. As I stared deep into his blue eyes, I sank down with agonizing slowness.

Watching the pleasure chase across his face was breathtaking. He sighed my name and clutched me tighter until he was buried to the hilt.

"I love you, Walker," I breathed, moving my hips and pressing my forehead to his. "When I was trapped in that nightmare, it was memories of you that got me through."

"River, Christ. You can't say shit like that to me. I'm gonna cry."

I kissed him, rolling my hips and grinding down with every stroke. He reached between us and ran his thumb over my clit in tight circles, urging me to an orgasm.

"I'm fucking close, baby. I need you to squeeze my cock and milk every last drop. Can you do that? Can you come for me?"

A shiver of pleasure took over my body, and the climax I hadn't quite reached came barreling in like a freight train. "God, Walker. So good."

He tensed, and his cock swelled inside me, pulsing with his release as he shuddered and groaned, holding on to me like I was going to disappear.

Afterward, when we were lying together in the big unfamiliar bed, he kissed my forehead and whispered, "I love you, River. More than I could've ever imagined when we were those two little kids chasing lightning bugs in the pasture."

Eyes wet with tears, I pulled back just enough to meet his gaze. "Enough to give me all the orange Starbursts in the pack?"

"Don't get crazy now."

I laughed as he squeezed me. "You already know I'd give you everything I have. My favorite candy. The shirt off my back. My dying breath. Whatever you need, darlin', it's yours."

"All I need is you."

His smile was tired, but no less sweet because of it. "Good, 'cause I've been yours since the day I first saw you."

"Liar, you were like four."

"God's honest truth, ladybug. You were my first love—and my last."

sixteen

• • •

Bishop

River had been soundly asleep for the last two hours since I'd taken over for Walker. He hadn't wanted to leave her, but Cross wanted to talk to him about the next steps with Volkov. Pretty sure that was the only excuse that would have pulled him from her bed this early.

I'd drawn the blackout curtains as soon as the sunlight began creeping in through the window, and now I sat in the corner, watching the woman I loved sleep. Sure, I could've gone to her and slipped into bed beside her, but that meant my guard would be down. I'd get wrapped up in her, and someone might come after her again.

It was safer this way. Me across the room in a chair standing guard, her in bed mostly peaceful. Okay, that was a lie. Her sleep, from what I could tell, had been far from peaceful. Every ten minutes or so, her fingers would twitch, and her expression would scrunch up in an anxious frown. No stranger to them myself, I recognized the symptoms of her nightmares. She was most likely reliving the time she'd spent in that hell she'd been trapped in.

Unfortunately, I also knew I couldn't just wake her up with a gentle shake of the arm. Any unwanted or unexpected touch was liable to send her over the edge. It's why I'd started humming nonsensical lullabies. As soon as she registered my voice, she settled back down.

"No . . . n-no, please." Her cry broke through the silence in the room, and my heart stuttered as she thrashed in bed.

"Bear. Stop. Bear, please don't go."

"Fuck," I rasped, pushing out of my chair and crossing to her. "It's okay, siren. You're okay. I'm right here."

Her breaths came in rapid, labored pants while she struggled, a tear slipping down her cheek and a sob breaking free.

I couldn't fucking do this. Leave her at the mercy of her subconscious.

"Open your eyes, River. I've got you. You're safe."

My hand hesitated beside hers on the bed, my fingers trembling as I battled my own monsters. You'd think it would be easy for me, touching her, especially after scaling a damn wall with her legs wrapped around my bare torso. It wasn't. If anything, the mere thought of her skin against mine sent my body breaking out in a cold sweat.

Then I had the excuse of the mission to focus on. It had been a literal matter of life and death. But here in this room, with nothing but the sounds of both of our demons crowding our minds, there was no escape from the memories. My nightmares were closer to the surface than ever, phantom hands ghosting across my body, inflicting never-ending torture.

I had to swallow back a wave of nausea and focus on the woman in front of me. It felt like I was clawing tooth and nail to get back to her, but dammit, she needed me. If there was anyone I could do this for, it was her. I couldn't leave her like this.

When she cried out again, I sat on the edge of the bed and reached out, bracing myself for the worst when I gently ran my fingertips over her forehead. Thankfully no fists came flying my way, though truth be told they would have hurt less than the tortured look hiding in her big green eyes as she blinked up at me.

"Sterling?" she asked, voice broken. "You're here."

"It was a nightmare, siren. That's all."

Her lower lip trembled. "No, it wasn't."

I frowned before I caught her meaning. She'd been reliving Bear's death.

I cursed inwardly, wishing I could spare her that truth. Since I couldn't do anything about Bear, I gave her what I could. "You're safe now, back here with us."

A shudder ran through her, but it didn't stop. Her whole body shivering, she wrapped her arms around herself and fought to control her breath.

"Scoot over," I murmured.

"What?"

"You heard me."

She did as I asked, and without another thought, I stripped down to my boxer briefs before sliding in beside her. I turned on my side, and she did the same, mirroring my movements but not attempting to close the distance I'd left between us.

We were maybe an inch apart, close enough that I was practically breathing in the air she exhaled. There was something about the thought that she was providing the air in my lungs that unlocked the last of the chains holding me.

"Come here, siren."

She blinked at me, her surprise unmistakable even in the darkness of the room. "Are you sure?"

"Put your hands on me. I know you need this just as much as I do." I hadn't willingly asked another person to touch me since *that* night, but River changed something inside me. For the first time in a long time, I wanted to feel someone else's skin against mine. Not just someone's.

Hers.

My siren.

The first woman who made me want to be Sterling, not just Bishop. The woman who took the ragged and torn pieces of me and carefully put them back in place. I may never again be the man that I'd once been, but for her, I could fucking try.

The first brush of her fingertips over my heart sent goosebumps erupting down my arms.

"Is this okay?" she whispered, mistaking my flinch for revulsion.

"Yeah. Just go slow." The last thing I wanted was for her to stop, even if panic was right behind the pleasure.

She leaned forward, replacing her fingers with her lips and brushing the gentlest kiss against my chest. A low groan escaped me. God, her barely there touches felt so fucking good. Despite her gentleness, every caress was like an electric current buzzing along my skin. I almost couldn't stand it, but in the same breath never wanted it to end.

"Your heart's beating so fast." She backed away and returned her head to her pillow, eyes locked on mine.

"Because of you."

"Do you need me to stop?" River pulled away, the lack of her warmth instantly noticeable.

I let out a low growl of protest as I snatched her hand and put it on me again, where it fucking belonged. "No."

Slowly, she dragged her nails across my collarbone, sending shivers down my spine. I didn't say a damn word as I held her gaze and reached out, mimicking her movements.

"Your skin's so soft, siren. Soft and perfect."

"So's yours."

It wasn't. Not even close. I had more scars on me than I did smooth patches, but fuck if I was going to correct her. She made me feel whole. That was all that mattered.

She spread her palm across my pec, her heat a comfort I wasn't used to feeling from another person, but now I couldn't imagine living without it.

Silently, I did the same to her, sliding the sheet down to her waist and baring her beautiful body to me. River might not ever truly understand how much she anchored me, and if I was honest, I didn't want her to bear the burden of that knowledge.

Hand skating across my chest, she watched my expression with rapt attention. The familiar curl of panic built inside me, one I wanted desperately to fight. I wouldn't let this be ruined, not when I finally had her safe in my arms.

"Sterling," she whispered, her focus never leaving me. "It's just us here. No one else."

I took a long breath as her fingers drew slow circles along my skin, mine repeating the movement over her breast. "No one else."

"I missed you, Sterling. All of you."

Leaning in, I ran my nose along hers as she let her palm map out the ridges of my abs. I was enjoying this game of ours far too much to stop now, even if she was dangerously close to one of my uglier scars. A distant part of my brain worried she might ask about them, but she didn't hesitate over the various bumps and blemishes. She just held my gaze as her hand traveled lower, halting when she skimmed the waistband of my boxers.

I nipped her bottom lip, my hand once again mimicking the same path hers took. Except where she'd met fabric, all I found was the cleft between her thighs. Wet, warm, and all fucking mine.

She whimpered when I ran my finger over her clit in slow circles.

"Take these off," she demanded, fingers inching below the elastic. "I want to touch you."

"Maybe right now I'd rather focus on touching you."

Parting her thighs a little, she welcomed me. "You *are* touching me."

"Not nearly enough," I whispered as I sank one digit into her, groaning at the heat that gripped me, wishing it was my cock.

"I've fantasized about the day it was me buried deep inside you, making you cry out for me as I fucked you and filled this perfect pussy."

"God, Sterling. The mouth on you. It should come with a warning label."

My fingers stilled, and I pulled back just far enough to catch her gaze. "Oh yeah? What would it say?"

"May cause spontaneous orgasms."

"I'd prefer they be intentional and plentiful. I don't do anything by accident. Except . . ." I stopped myself from saying the words. Was this the right time? The right way? I'd never confessed anything close to this to a woman before.

Her brow furrowed, eyes searching as she waited for me to finish. Finally she asked, "Except what?"

The truth was, all we had was right fucking now. If I didn't tell her and something happened, I'd regret it for the rest of my life, or she'd live out her days never knowing how I felt. "Except for falling in love with you. I didn't plan that, but it happened all the same, and I wouldn't do a damn thing to change it."

"Sterling—"

I kissed her, cutting off whatever else she'd been about to say. I didn't need the words. I saw the proof of her feelings for me in the gentle way she touched me. How she waited for my cues and never pushed me farther than I was comfortable going. Her heart may not belong solely to me, but it was no less *mine*.

Pushing her onto her back, I fitted myself between her welcoming thighs and hovered over her, lips taking what I wanted in long, drugging kisses. She reached down and worked my boxers over my hips, freeing my aching length as she did.

I slid the weeping crown of my cock through her slick folds and had to fight the urge to spread her legs wider and drive in deep.

"Let me in, siren. I want to fuck you bare and so deep you'll feel me for days."

"God, yes."

Rising on my knees, I adjusted our position until her legs were on my shoulders, that pink cunt open and on full display.

"Can I touch you?" she asked, her hand hovering between us.

"Anywhere but my back."

I wasn't quite ready for us to test out that minefield of past trauma. Things were going so well, and I didn't want anything to ruin this moment for us. Best to play it safe for now. We'd save that for another time.

Nodding to show she understood, she planted her palms on my thighs, her fingernails digging in when I took myself in my hand and ran my cock over her clit. Her desperate little mewls made me smile, and before I gave her what she wanted, I delivered a sharp slap to her cunt using only my dick.

"Fuck, Sterling. Do it again, please."

"You look so good begging for my cock, baby."

And she did, her blonde hair splayed on the pillow, cheeks flushed, pupils blown. She was already half-gone to pleasure, and I wasn't even inside her yet.

I dragged the head of my dick across her until I was notched at her entrance, fucking desperate to sink home but somehow holding myself back. Using every ounce of control I had, I rocked my hips forward, barely breaching her heat.

"You are such a fucking tease," she groaned, her nails sinking into my thighs again.

The walls of her pussy fluttered around me like she was trying to suck me inside, and it was all I could do to hold back.

"Haven't you ever played just the tip, beautiful?"

"I'm not known for my patience."

Without warning, she lifted her hips and took me all the way to the root.

"Fuck, baby. I . . . God, you feel good." I had to grit my teeth against the unreal sensation of her clenched tight around my shaft. "Better than I imagined."

"You imagined it?"

"Often and with great relish."

"Oh yeah? And what did you do while you imagined it?"

"Fucked my fist and pretended it was you."

"Good thing you don't have to pretend anymore."

"Damn right," I said, pressing in just a hint deeper, using her position to my advantage.

River gasped. "Christ, you feel good."

"That's my line."

"Doesn't make it any less true."

Rolling my pelvis, I sank in until I reached as far as possible, coming up against her cervix and making her moan.

"Fuck me, Sterling."

I couldn't help but grin down at her as my hand slid from her ankle down to her knee. "Oh baby, you asked for it."

Without warning, I began driving in hard and deep, our angle ensuring I hit the spot inside her that made her gush over and over. River's cries only just drowned out the sound of our skin slapping together as we chased our combined releases.

"Fuck, baby, I'm gonna come," I warned.

"Don't stop. Don't stop."

"Come with me."

"I'm right there."

"Touch yourself. I need you to milk my cock for all it's worth."

Reaching between her legs, she barely brushed her clit before her cunt squeezed me like a vise and she screamed my name. That was it. I was over the cliff and spilling inside her, vision gone white with pleasure.

"Fuck, Sterling, I love you," she panted, eyes holding mine as we came back down.

I adjusted our bodies, carefully repositioning her legs so they were around my waist without pulling free of her. I wasn't ready to leave her warmth just yet. Lowering myself so I could hover over her again, I kissed her forehead, her cheek, then finally her pillowy lips. I didn't want to lose this moment.

She shifted beneath me, freeing one of her arms so she could slide it up and around my neck until her fingers threaded through my hair. I shivered, the soft touch sending tingles all through my body.

My dick gave a happy twitch inside her, no more immune to the touch than the rest of me.

She froze and then giggled. "Already?"

"What can I say? It's been a while. And my shift with you is just getting started."

"Your shift?"

"We're taking turns watching over you."

"This is your version of watching over me."

"You complaining, siren?"

"Fuck no, just checking." She rolled her hips and made us both groan as I hardened all over again. "I think I need you to watch me harder."

"My pleasure, ma'am. I live to serve."

"Is that the SEAL motto?"

"Might as well be," I muttered, rolling us until she was seated on top of me.

"How do you feel about overtime?"

I cocked a brow. "You mean staying past my shift?"

"I do now."

I chuckled. "You looking for a two-for-one special, baby girl?"

Her pussy clenched around me.

"I'll take that as a yes."

Grabbing her hips, I encouraged her to move in slow circles as I stared at her in absolute wonder.

"Three," she gasped, grinding down on me. "Three-for-one. I always want all three of you, Sterling."

Smirking, I reached up and tweaked one rosy nipple. "I'll see what I can do."

seventeen

• • •

Cross

I sat outside with a steaming mug of coffee, the morning mist heavy over the lake, water still as glass, birdsong filling the air. Fucking idyllic. At least it would've been for anyone else.

There was nothing magical or perfect about my current situation. At best, I was sitting in the eye of the storm.

Instead of the peaceful call of doves, the sounds of River's pleasured moans echoed in my mind. I'd stood outside the bedroom door like a fucking fool listening to Bishop fuck my wife, hand poised to knock, cock hard and heart racing while my body and mind waged war. One screamed at me to join them, knowing from past experience they'd both welcome me. The other couldn't find a single reason she'd want me in there.

What would she see when she finally looked me in the eye? The man who'd lost her. Who'd let her friend die. The husband she'd been shackled to against her will? The one who'd abandoned her without so much as a backward glance after she'd given him her heart? I may have rescued her from Volkov, but she wouldn't have been in his sights if it hadn't been for me.

River didn't owe me a goddamn thing, let alone a second chance.

I'd ruined her life at every turn. Even without fucking trying.

Heaving a sigh, I drained my coffee and stood, itching to do something more. I needed to see her, even if it meant watching her with Bishop. After everything we'd been through, I needed that moment of reconnection with her. That split second when our eyes locked would tell me everything I needed to know about whose name was written on her heart. I'd know if I belonged there. If I was welcome. If I deserved her love too.

With purposeful strides, I made my way through the sprawling estate, not stopping until I reached the bedroom door. It was ajar, the low murmur of voices from the room telling me Walker and Bishop were inside. With her.

"It's not your shift, Walker," Bishop said on a sigh.

"So fucking what? Is there some blood oath I don't know about? A goddamned secret password?"

"No."

"My point exactly. Now scoot over and make room."

Bishop grumbled about him being a selfish asshole and did as he was told. River made a sleepy sound as he pulled away, but my brother was right there to comfort her. "Hush, darlin'. I'm here."

I watched as my brother pulled off his shirt and tossed it aside before slipping in behind her. Her happy little noise and the way she took his hand and draped it over her waist while pillowing her head on Bishop's arm was a punch to the gut. Fuck, I wanted to be the one holding her like that.

Bishop stared at her with stars in his damn eyes as he gently stroked the side of her face. "Go back to sleep, siren. We've got you. Nothing's gonna hurt you ever again."

Walker kissed her nape, adding a soft, "Only sweet dreams from here on out, ladybug. We'll chase away all the others."

"Mmm, love you," she murmured.

My heart gave a painful lurch at the happy picture the three of them painted.

The fed was right. He and Walk did have her. More than that, she was happy with the two of them. Hell, she just said she loved them. It wasn't exactly like she was asking anyone where I was.

There was no missing puzzle piece here. Just one that didn't fit.

I was right to come looking for her.

I got the answer I needed.

It just wasn't the one I was hoping for.

Goddamn, that realization was a hell of a lot more painful than I'd expected.

Before either Bishop or Walker noticed me hovering in the doorway like a voyeur, I turned away and left them to their love nest. Pieces of my broken heart rained down with every step. I pulled out my phone and opened the email I'd steadfastly ignored for the better part of two months. As much as I didn't want to lose her, I knew there was only one way I could ever truly have her. I had to set my sparrow free.

For good this time.

Opening McCreedy's message, my eyes skimmed over his brief but damning: *In case you change your mind.*

And then a little further down to the attachment titled: *Petition for Divorce.*

My hand shook as I downloaded the document and read over the details. I didn't fucking want this, but if it meant she could be happy, I'd give it to her. I'd give her anything.

Finger hovering over the print icon, I debated my choice for one more heartbeat. But the picture of the three of them happy together, brought together by free will and nothing more, flashed in my head. I wanted her to choose me without a single doubt.

I pressed print.

Walker

"EITHER YOU ANSWER your fucking phone or I'm throwing it out the window," Bishop grumbled, giving my shoulder a rough shove before gently cradling his hand over River's ear.

"I just fell asleep. Whoever it is can wait."

"Apparently they can't, because they're blowing your shit up."

"Five more minutes," I groaned.

"Walker, I swear to God, if she wakes up because of your phone, it's gonna be your ass going out the window."

I let out a begrudging sigh and slipped out of bed, instantly mourning the feel of River pressed against me.

"What the fuck do you want, Tex? I'm busy."

Bishop glared at me and made a shooing motion with his hand. I flipped him off, but gave him my back in the barest gesture of obedience. There was no way in hell I was leaving this room. He was the one who wanted me to take the call. He could fucking deal with it.

And if River woke up, well, we'd just have to see about helping her fall back to a blissed-out sleep. With our dicks.

Win fucking win.

"Where are you? Y'all missed the vet's visit this morning. You never miss that. I had to fill in for you."

Shit. That's right. We had a whole ranch we were supposed to be running. Instead we'd been stealing our woman from the fucking Bratva.

"We had to pick River up. We'll be back soon. Can you handle things on the ranch until we get home?"

"I suppose. Does this mean I'll be getting overtime?"

"Yeah, sure, whatever." I raked a hand through my hair, annoyed as fuck that this asshole interrupted my time with River for something as insignificant as a vet visit. "I gotta go, Tex. You have it handled?"

"Well, actually, now that you mention it, I've got a few issues I need to run by you. Shouldn't take but a few minutes."

"No. Text me what you need, or better yet, text Cross. I've been up all night. I need some shuteye."

"Wait, wait, wait. Before you hang up—"

"This better be important, or you can kiss that overtime goodbye. I'll put you on castration duty."

"Your golden boy is missing. Figured you should know."

I stilled, fear that Volkov was going after our people taking hold of me. "What? Who's my golden boy?"

"Bishop. He hightailed it out of here as soon as y'all were gone. Left us high and dry. Unless you . . . took him to the train station?"

My knees about gave out on me, and I had to press a palm against the wall to keep myself upright. "Oh. That. No, he, uh, had a family emergency or something. Asked to take a couple days off."

"Emergency, huh? Hope everything's all right."

"Yeah, didn't sound like anyone was dying."

"What?"

"Uh, I just meant it seems like he had it in hand." Fuck, I was rambling. I got sloppy when I rambled. "Like I said, Tex, talk to Cross if you've got any more issues. I'm dead on my feet."

I hung up before he could say another word, my gut a ball of worry. He'd asked too many questions about Bishop, and I'd flailed like a flag in a damn hurricane. Or worse, one of those sky dancers at the car dealerships, with their wacky arms and permanently shocked expressions.

"You about done?" Bishop asked.

"Yeah. We didn't exactly have time to let the crew know we were going MIA."

"Why'd I hear my name?"

"They noticed you were gone. You had a family emergency, by the way."

"Shit," he swore. "Thanks for covering for me."

I shrugged, turning my phone on silent. "It's the truth, more or less."

River stirred, her eyes fluttering open as she rolled over and looked at me. "Where's Cross?"

I smiled at her before tossing my phone on the side table as I approached. "He's doing boring businessman shit, darlin'. Don't worry. He's close by. How are you?"

"Sleepy."

Bishop gave me a smug grin. "I wore her out."

"Only 'cause I had her first."

River let out a huff that was too sleepy to be a laugh. "Okay, boys, no fighting, or I'll kick you out and cuddle with Cross."

I faked a shudder as I caught Bishop's silver stare. "I think she just threatened to go get Daddy."

"He is not now, nor will he ever be, my daddy." Bishop wrapped his arm around River and tugged her back until she was against him.

"I want to see him," she murmured through a yawn.

"You will." I pressed a kiss to her nose.

Bishop nipped her shoulder and rumbled, "After you get some more sleep. We're not going anywhere."

"Promise?"

I didn't let him answer her. I cupped her cheek and pressed our foreheads together. "Cross my heart, darlin'. We just fought like hell to get you back. No way are we letting you go again."

eighteen

• • •

River

Slipping out of bed as quietly as possible so I didn't disturb Walker, I tiptoed to the dresser where my borrowed clothes waited. A pair of sweats and a soft T-shirt. Perfect. The soft, clean cotton felt like heaven after weeks of living in my own filth.

The light coming from under the bathroom door and the faint sound of running water told me Bishop was showering. The man had probably gone for a run while Walker and I were passed out. He didn't sleep much on a good night, and I couldn't blame him. I thought I understood before, but now that I'd seen firsthand what horrors Volkov and his goons were capable of, I realized just how naïve I'd really been. That I could sleep at all was a miracle.

Honestly, if not for Bishop and Walker being there to soothe me every time the memories hit, I might not have.

Darkness encroached on the relative peace I'd found. My skin no longer felt clean, and anxiety danced in my veins. What would happen when they weren't there? It wasn't like I could count on them to babysit me while I slept every night. Eventually I would be left alone. What then?

These thoughts were chased by another. The one that had finally pulled me from the comfort of Walker's arms.

Why hadn't Cross come to check on me?

Was it because he saw me in that auction? A piece of meat for others to scrutinize and devour. Was I tainted in his eyes now?

Daniel Cross Jr. never settled for damaged goods. Not in his business. Not in his life.

The men at that auction may have been wearing masks, but I knew they were the same men who would sit across from him at a conference table or work alongside him on some business deal.

Seeing him walk into an event with me on his arm, he'd be a laughingstock. The billionaire rancher with a whore for a wife.

I shuddered, each ugly thought worse than the last.

If I could just see him, hold him, I knew it would calm the worst of my fears.

With a glance over my shoulder at Walker, still sleeping peacefully, I opened the bedroom door and crept into the hallway. If I knew my husband, he'd be awake and working on something by now. Relaxing was rarely part of his routine, at least from what I'd seen. Even when I was a kid, aware of him as I was, I'd noticed the way he kept himself occupied. Whether it was working on the ranch or handling paperwork, Cross had always been too busy to pay me any attention. Although now I wondered how much of that was intentional.

Walker and Bishop had both made time to check on me. He might be the head of an empire, but surely Cross could spare ten minutes to do the same?

Now I wasn't sure if I was hurt or angry, but of the two, anger was easier. It didn't give me room to wallow in self-pity, so anger it was.

I hadn't paid much attention when Walker'd brought me up here last night, not that it would have made a difference; the place was massive. Anything short of a 'You Are Here' sign on the wall wouldn't have helped me find my way around. I sure as shit wasn't going to wander the halls calling his name. So I opted for exploration, my favorite way to learn my surroundings.

He had to be here somewhere. Even if he didn't want me anymore, he wouldn't just abandon us. Would he?

A little voice in my head whispered, *He's done it before.*

The immediate twist of pain in my heart had a soft gasp escaping before I could stop myself.

No. Stop. It. He had a reason then. And he literally just snuck into an illegal auction and tried to pay a million dollars to get you back. That is not the move of a guy looking to run the other way.

I shook my head to clear my mind of those intrusive thoughts. Cross didn't deserve my doubt. He'd more than made up for our past. God, the man had groveled on an epic scale. I knew how much of his pride he'd had to give up in order to do that. He'd all but been on his knees.

"Cross?" I asked as I poked my head into what looked like an office.

This one was by far more tasteful than the one at the ranch. I mean, just the fact that there wasn't an ostentatious portrait of Ransom hanging dead center on the wall said a lot. And without further inspection, there was no way to know whether it was hiding a secret passage of its own. Something told me our host wouldn't appreciate me sleuthing on that scale, though I had to admit the temptation was high.

My favorite part was the breathtaking view of the lake. A small yacht was moored at the dock, the bright blue sky reflecting off the water promising summer days without a care in the world. This really was a peaceful retreat. Maybe one day I could convince the guys we needed a place like this to get away from it all. The things we could get up to on a boat . . .

I was stalling; I could admit it. Cross wasn't here, and I was using the view as a way to keep myself distracted as my anxiety ravaged me. Turning away from the window, I made for the door, shifting to avoid the meticulously organized printing center nearby. But something stopped me, a tendril of recognition drawing me to the papers sitting face up in the print tray.

The words *Petition for Divorce* stood out like a beacon, calling to me. Ransom was married? I shouldn't have given in to my curiosity. This wasn't any of my business, but I was a nosy bitch.

The second I read the words on the pilfered page, I wished I'd never set eyes on them.

In re the Marriage of:

Daniel Everett Cross Junior, PETITIONER

AND

River Danielle Adams, RESPONDENT

Oh.
My.
God.
That fucking coward.
He was running. Again.

Cross

WHAT THE FUCK had I done? I'd just lit the fuse on my marriage and didn't even know where I'd sent the fucking bomb.

Gut churning, hands shaking, I pocketed my phone and headed off in search of Ransom. It was his damn house. He'd be able to tell me where the printer was.

I found him in the kitchen, sitting at the breakfast nook with a crossword puzzle, a pen, and a carafe of coffee beside him.

"Why do you look like you took a kick straight to the junk, Danny boy?" Ransom asked, eyes going wide at the state of me.

"I need to know where your office is."

"Hold up a minute. Just take a breath." He gestured toward a buffet of pastries and fruit. "Maybe grab yourself a muffin or something. Jesus. You're making me twitchy."

"I don't have time for a goddamned muffin."

He raised a mocking brow. "You got somewhere else to be? I

thought the whole point of coming out here was that you four were laying low. So pull up a chair and enjoy a fucking muffin."

Sighing, I grabbed one out of the basket on the island and took a seat across from him. My stomach was in knots, but I forced myself to take a begrudging bite. The sweet burst of blueberry and vanilla was a pleasant surprise, so I took another. "Happy?"

"Nope. What is wrong with you? You've got your girl. You should be celebrating, or smiling at the very least." Pouring himself a fresh cup, he offered the carafe to me, but I shook my head. "Honestly, with the way you watched every move she made, I'm surprised you're not with her right now."

"It's better if she's with them. She's happy with them."

His eyes went wide, and he choked on his coffee but recovered quickly. "Them?"

"It's complicated."

"I'd say. She's your wife, ain't she?"

My chest tightened as a thought flickered through my brain. *Not for much longer.* "Legally speaking."

He frowned at me. "So how's that work?"

"We don't exactly have a playbook. It just does. Did. Fuck."

Ransom scratched his cheek, looking dubious. "And you think she's happy with them but not you?"

"All I've ever done is get her hurt. She tried to get away from me, but I just shoved my way into her life, and look at what happened."

"What did happen? You didn't give me much to go on when you asked to come stay here."

"It's for the best. The less you know, the less you're implicated."

"Great," he muttered, taking another swig of his coffee. "I'll just make sure McCreedy's retainer is paid through the end of the year."

"He's already well aware of our situation."

"For fuck's sake, what did you get me into, Cross?"

"Nothing you can't buy your way out of."

Ransom held my stare and then grinned. "True. So continue. You were in the middle of giving me your sob story about how you ruined your girl's life. Though, I gotta tell you, Cross, from where I'm sitting, that's not the way it looks."

"What do you mean?"

"She's head over heels for you, man. I saw it at the gala, and again last night. That woman is so attuned to you. All three of you, now that I think of it, which makes more sense knowing you're all . . ." He trailed off, fishing for info I wasn't going to provide. Clearing his throat, he continued, "Right. Anyway, she might be the sun you three orbit around, but your pull on her is just as strong. It's gravity, man. You're lucky. That's not easy to come by, and it's even easier to lose. Especially for men in our position."

His gaze dropped to the table, then lifted to meet mine again, a haunted look in his eyes now. "Trust me, I should know."

I didn't want to be here right now, sitting at a fucking breakfast nook eating a goddamn blueberry muffin—I didn't even like blueberries—and having a heart-to-heart with Brett Ransom about the great love of my life. But he was right on one point. A love like hers wasn't easy to come by.

And maybe I'd been a little hasty pushing that button.

"As lovely as this domestic fucking moment has been, I really need to find your printer. Where is it?"

Ransom chuckled, then said, "My office. Down the hall, third door on the left."

"Thanks."

Pushing to my feet, I snagged what was left of my pastry and chucked it in the bin by the door on my way out, leaving Ransom to his crossword and memories.

If I wasn't in the middle of my own crisis, I'd probably have given more thought to what had put that look in his eyes. I knew he'd had a very public breakup with some socialite he'd been engaged to years back, but we weren't the type to bare our souls to one another, so I'd never gotten his take on it.

Either way, it wasn't my problem.

Right now, I just needed to find those papers, tear them up, and go talk to my girl. I'd give her a choice before I did a damn thing to end our marriage.

Counting doors, I tore through the hall toward Ransom's office, desperate to wipe away any remnants of my doubt in us. If I got rid of the papers, I never had to tell River they existed. Just because they were drafted didn't mean anything. It wasn't like they were filed. Or like I even asked McCreedy to draw them up in the first place. He'd done that on his own.

Fueled with righteous purpose, I stormed inside, only to stop dead.

River was in front of the window, posture rigid, hands shaking, a single piece of paper held between them.

God really must fucking hate me. And after the things I'd done, I couldn't blame him. I was hardly a pious member of his flock. I bet he was sitting up there on a damn cloud, laughing at the coincidence he set into motion.

"It's not what it looks like," was my feeble response, the words sounding as cliché as they were.

Her eyes lifted to mine, a single tear rolling down her cheek. "It looks like you want a divorce."

"River, I—"

"Save your breath. I don't need you to tell me why. I should have expected this." Her voice shook, and it nearly brought me to my knees. "I just . . . God, I thought we were better. I thought we'd gotten past the games and lies and fucking betrayals. Did any of it matter to you? Was any of it real? Not the marriage, obviously. That's been a joke from the start. But the rest of it? You and me?"

Nausea clutched at my stomach, a pit forming there, cold and unforgiving. "Sparrow, you don't understand. I thought it would be better to let you have a say."

"Oh, that's big of you. And did my say come before you signed this? Or were you going to wait until after I was served? At what point, exactly, do I get a say, Cross?"

"River, I . . ." I shook my head, at a total loss. I never actually expected to have this conversation. My world was falling apart around me, and I'd never felt so unprepared in my entire life.

"You let me think we were happy. The things you said . . . You came to find me. What was the point if you were just going to let me go?"

"We were happy."

"But not anymore? What changed?"

God, I was fucking this up.

"You never wanted to be married to me, sparrow."

"Would you stop telling me what I want?" She was angry now. Good. I could deal with her angry. I knew how to fight back when her temper got the better of her.

"It's the truth, dammit. You never meant to marry me. Nothing about our lives together has gone the way it was supposed to. You deserve to choose. I want you to choose. Dammit, River. For once, I want you to choose me. Not because you were fucking forced into it by my manipulative fucking father."

"Open your eyes. I chose you. Every day I chose you. I stayed, didn't I?"

"Because you had to."

"I could have filed for divorce right away, but I didn't. I stayed married to you instead."

"Because Bishop convinced you to."

"Because I loved you! Even when I tried to convince myself I hated you."

"And I'm letting you go because I love you." Fuck, I hated how my voice broke on those last words.

She stared at me, eyes swimming with angry tears she'd fight tooth and nail to keep from spilling over. "If that's the truth, then why didn't you come to me after we got here? Why did you leave me with them and print fucking divorce papers?"

A shuddering sigh escaped me as I let my walls down. She deserved my honesty. It was all I could give her. "I failed you. As a protector, as a husband, as the man who loves you. How can you even stand to look at me right now, sparrow? They took you because I wasn't the man you needed. Because I couldn't take the fucking shot."

Her eyes softened infinitesimally, but her words were just as scathing as before. "Because you could have shot me. Don't you get it, you idiot? You *were* protecting me. You have been ever since you wrote me that stupid note. You don't always go about it the right way, but from the moment you decided I was yours, you've always put me first."

"You're right. Which is why I printed these damn papers."

She shoved me in the chest, pushing said papers against me.

"When are you going to start *asking* me before you make decisions about my life? Or does being yours mean I don't get a say?"

"That's the whole point. It should be your choice to be married to me or not. Hell, you said as much yourself not all that long ago in the gazebo."

She threw her head back and let out a disbelieving laugh. "Oh my God, do you not see how fucked up this situation is? You want me to choose, so you decide we're getting divorced without even discussing it with me? Way to miss the entire fucking point. You are the most infuriating man I've ever known."

"Christ, you're such a stubborn pain in my ass," I grumbled, but there wasn't any real anger there. She was touching me, her palm on my chest, body so close all I'd need to do was dip my head and claim her lips.

"And you're a pain in mine."

"Last chance to get out, River. What do you want?"

Her breath hitched, palm tensing over the documents pressed against my sternum. "I don't want to lose this."

Snatching the papers from her, I held her stare as I tore them down the middle, letting both halves fall to the floor. "You're stuck with me now."

"You're stuck with me."

Crooking a finger through the neck of her shirt, I tugged her hard until she tumbled into me. "Good."

Then my lips were on hers, and there was no more talking. She tore at my belt like a woman possessed, her kisses as frantic and hungry as mine. I'd fucking yearned for her every moment she was gone, and now that I had her in my arms, I expected that feeling to wane. It didn't. It was an ache deep inside me, a well I couldn't fill fast enough. I'd never have enough of her.

"I need you inside me," she panted.

Hoisting her up, I carried her to the desk, pausing only long enough to sweep my arm across the slab of oak and send Ransom's shit clattering to the floor before setting her down.

She giggled. "Oh man, Gigi is going to lose her mind when she hears about this. Totally a scene straight outta her books."

"Remind me to talk to you about Gigi later. Much later. Like tomorrow." Her eyes flashed with a question, but I stopped her by yanking her sweats off and baring that pink pussy to me. "Do you know how much I crave you, baby?"

"Are you talking to me or her?"

"Why can't it be both?"

That little giggle again. I lived for that fucking giggle.

She reached for me, working on my zipper and tugging my Wranglers down my hips. "Only fair I get to look at you." My dick sprang free, and she cooed. "Hello, lover."

Lifting her thin T-shirt, I pulled the fabric over her head so I could suck one tight nipple into my mouth. The way she whimpered and arched into me sent a punch of feral need through me, and I groaned against her breast.

"Cross, don't tease me."

"You're not the one in charge here, sparrow." I grinned at her huff a second before I placed my palm on her chest and shoved her back. "Now be a good girl and take what I give you."

"Sir, yes, sir."

"You are such a fucking brat."

"You love it."

"I love you."

Her eyes went soft. "I love you too."

My cock was fucking weeping for her. A drop of precum beaded at the tip as I stroked myself once from base to crown. "Open for me, wife. Let me in."

She propped herself on her elbows and watched, knees falling open, eyes trained on my dick as I rubbed myself through her wet slit. "Cross," she whined, but it cut off on a moan when I pressed the head inside her.

I held her heated stare and then purposefully looked down at where we were barely joined. "Watch," I demanded.

She pushed herself up just enough, and when I was sure she could see, I started to slide into her. We were both breathing hard, the deliberately slow glide driving us both insane.

"Cross, hurry."

"No fucking way." I was panting with the effort it took to restrain myself. "I'm not rushing a damn thing."

Hooking her legs around my hips, she tried to pull me forward and bring me deeper inside her. I stopped her with a warning look. "You'll take my dick however I want to give it, sparrow."

"Then give it to me," she growled. "I need you, Cross. I need to feel you. I need you to fuck me."

The unspoken words were just under her carnal demand. She wanted me to help her forget. To replace the horrors with new, better memories. To know without a doubt that I didn't want her any less after the things that had happened. Just like Walker and Bishop had done.

"Fuck," I groaned. "I need you too. But look at your pretty cunt taking my thick dick, sweetness. Just like you were made to."

I had about an inch to go, and sweat was beading down my spine. It felt like I'd run a marathon when all I'd actually done was force myself not to drive in all the way to the root. Who knew restraint could be so taxing?

"Fuck me full of you, Cross." She wriggled her hips. "I want your cum leaking out of me for the rest of the day."

My cock jerked. "You know what you're asking for, sparrow? I know you haven't had your pill since they took you."

Her eyes locked on mine as she nodded. "Don't pull out. I want your cum inside me, Cross. Where it belongs."

Fuck.

There was no holding back after that. I slammed the last little bit inside her, immediately drawing back and slamming in again.

"That breeding kink'll get ya every time," she said with a breathy laugh. "I should have started with that."

"And what if I fill you with more than my cum? You want to walk out of here full of my baby?"

Her nipples were hard little bullets as she rocked her hips against me. "I wouldn't be risking it if I didn't."

Jesus Christ. A tendril of something close to fear worked its way through me at the very real possibility I could knock her up.

I stopped myself from pulling out and sinking back inside. Instead

I kept us joined and stared down at the woman I loved. "You really want to risk bringing a child into this fucked up world?"

She reached up, her fingertips brushing over the damp skin of my chest, right above my heart. "Knowing that a little piece of us was out there in the world makes it worth the risk. That way, no matter what happens to us, we'll always be together. Somewhere."

"Fuck. Fuck."

I equal parts loved the sentiment but hated thinking about the possibility of us not being together. Scooping her off the desk, I carried her over to the window, pressing her back against the cool glass.

"What are you doing?" she asked, moaning as I sank deeper inside her.

"I want to fuck you where everyone can see it. I want everyone in this fucking state to know you're mine."

"I think that little news bulletin of yours did the trick."

Thrusting into her, I let out a ragged breath and fought the urge to come. "Don't care. Scream my name, baby. I want the message to stick."

"Cross, God, it's so deep."

"Take it. Come for me. Take everything I fucking have." My balls were throbbing with the need for release, my dick a length of steel as I staved off the urge to plant my seed inside her.

She was close, her walls gripping me hard, milking me as if they were begging me to do just that.

"Cross . . . oh, fuck."

"That's it, baby. Come for me. Scream my name. Let everyone fucking know who owns this pussy."

"Cross. Fuck. Cross."

I was pretty sure her nails had drawn blood with the way she clawed at me as she came.

"I love how pretty you come, sweetness. Give it to me."

She did. Cunt clamping down on me, she continued riding that wave of pleasure until mine followed in its wake.

"Fuck, I'm coming, River." Long pulses of euphoria radiated through me as I spilled jet after jet of my cum inside her. My knees trembled, threatening to give out from the force of my orgasm, but I wasn't ready for this to be over. I wanted to live like this, joined with my wife, giving her a piece of me.

My erection didn't flag as I slid out of her.

River blinked at me in surprise as I helped her stand. Without explanation, I spun her around, pressing her against the glass and resting my splayed palms over hers.

"Jesus, you're still hard?" she asked, grinding her ass into me.

"You gave me the green light, baby. I'm not stopping until the job is done."

"Fuck."

"Now you're getting it," I said with a grin, lining myself up with her slick cunt before sliding back into her. "Good girl."

nineteen

. . .

Bishop

My boots thumped on the dock as I walked to the edge, inspecting the boards while I went. Ransom might have assured me this place was secure, but I wouldn't believe it until I saw it all with my own eyes. There was too much on the line for me to slip up again.

My phone went off, startling me with the vibration in my pocket. I'd only just turned it on again about an hour ago. It showed hundreds of missed calls and messages, each one sending my career further down the drain. I'd gone off the grid. In the middle of a mission. It was career suicide.

I didn't give a fuck. Codes of conduct and mission parameters didn't mean shit to me right now. I'd have burned that house to the ground with every goddamn motherfucking piece of shit sorry excuse for a human inside. When it came to River, there was no line I wouldn't cross. I would sell my soul for that woman.

Every.

Single.

Time.

But I couldn't ignore Wilson any longer. Not if I wanted to put an end to this.

"Bishop," I barked, staring back at the house with dread in my gut.

They'd come for me. Throw me in some unmarked cell on a trumped-up charge of treason because of my betrayal if they could. I knew that, but River deserved more than a life running from my past.

It didn't matter what happened to me so long as she lived free. Walker and Cross would take care of her.

"You'd better be fucking dead and this is your goddamn ghost talking to me right now, Agent Bishop." Wilson's voice was a quiet storm.

"I'm not."

"Maybe you forgot how this works. You answer to me, motherfucker. You don't go AWOL. You check in. You report as scheduled. You do your fucking job."

"That's what I did."

"The hell you did. You disappeared without a word. Do you have any idea what we've been dealing with? The number of bodies you just left in your wake?"

"One."

"What?"

"One body."

And technically, it was River's kill.

"The fuck you did. It was a damn slaughterhouse. What the hell happened, Bishop?"

"I dunno. I didn't stick around."

"Where the fuck are you?"

"I can't tell you that."

He let out a humorless laugh. "He can't tell me, he says. We've got a fucking joker here." His voice dropped, going dark and serious. "Well, maybe this will get you to play ball, funny man. Volkov is gone, evaporated in thin air after torching our only lead. As far as I'm concerned, you've switched sides at this point. Don't make me bring you in. You're throwing it all away for a piece of ass."

"How would you know anything about me?"

"You think we haven't got eyes on you? The only reason I haven't pulled you out of there was that you were our link to Volkov and the Cross brothers. If you love her, you'll give them to us now."

"'Fraid I can't do that."

"You better think real carefully about what you are saying to me, Agent Bishop."

Swallowing thickly, I watched as Walker sat on the patio with River nestled against him, her head resting on his shoulder, a sweet smile on her face. Cross joined them, leaning against the railing that bordered the outdoor living space. She was happy, finally. I wasn't going to do anything to jeopardize that.

"I have."

"We have a lock on your location."

"Then why'd you ask me for it?"

"I was giving you a chance to come clean. Prove you weren't a traitor."

I gritted my teeth, the dig landing. I'd always been a patriot. I'd sacrificed everything and still bore the scars of my service. But I guess it wasn't my country that held my loyalty any longer. It was a River.

"They aren't the ones you want, sir. It's not the Cross brothers who'll see justice is served, and you know it."

"No, but they certainly have dirty enough hands to give us everything we need on Volkov."

"You don't need them," I insisted.

"Bring them in, Agent Bishop."

"I can't."

Wilson sighed. "Then I guess this means you'll be coming in with them."

"So be it."

"It doesn't have to be this way, Sterling," he said, his voice losing its edge. "You give them to us, you can keep her. We'll medically retire you, full pension, all the bells and whistles."

I wish I could say it wasn't tempting.

"Like I said, I can't. They're not taking the fall for something their father set in motion. They don't have a clue about the scope of the things he's done."

"But they profited off them, which makes them complicit. You know the laws. They're accomplices, whether they realized it or not."

River's laugh floated to me on the breeze, steeling my resolve. "I'm sorry, sir. I don't agree. And I don't think a jury will either."

His laugh was cruel. "You really think we'll allow you to testify?"

"No. But I have other ways of ensuring my evidence makes it into the right hands."

"You sonofabitch."

"I have as many friends as you, Wilson. More even, who owe me favors. Just because this isn't playing out the way you wanted doesn't mean I'm not prepared or a force to be reckoned with. Don't forget who I am."

"Who you *used* to be."

"Let me bring down Volkov before you use these men as your bargaining chips." I'd see justice for River and all the others Dominik and his goons had hurt, or I'd die trying.

"Catching him won't spare you."

"Doesn't matter. You can take all the credit if that makes you sleep better at night."

Wilson was quiet for several beats, likely mulling matters over in his mind. "Fine."

I was almost surprised he agreed, except I knew what a selfish bastard he was. He was after a promotion, and taking credit for Volkov's capture would almost certainly assure it.

"You know, Bishop, if we found you, so can he. Wouldn't be surprised if he was on his way to you and that pretty girl of yours right now."

Ice ran down my spine, my heart plummeting as I stared at River. "Do you know that for certain, or are you speculating?"

"We both know it only takes a single phone call to get a trace."

Fuck.

Walker took a call this morning.

We'd been so caught up in getting River we'd completely ignored the fact that there'd been a mole at the ranch.

Fuck.

"Wilson, I've got to go."

"I thought that might be your answer. You always were a good asset, Agent Bishop. It'll be a shame to lose you."

I hung up and sprinted for the patio, my heart in my throat.

We were so fucking stupid. I never should have let Walker take that call. I'd been distracted by River. Again.

What good were these skills of mine when I always seemed to forget my training when it mattered most?

"Whoa, where's the fire?" Walker asked, the grin on his face dying the instant he took in my expression.

"Who besides Walker has taken a call since we arrived?" I barked.

"What?" Walker asked.

"Who?" I nearly shouted this time.

River and Cross exchanged worried glances before she looked to me and shook her head. "Not me. I don't even have my phone."

"You?" I demanded, glaring at Cross.

"I checked my email. That's it."

I raked a hand through my hair and heaved a sigh. "Well, I guess that solves one mystery, then."

"You wanna back up and tell us what's going on, super spy?" Walker asked.

"Tex is your mole."

His brows flew up, and he let out a disbelieving laugh. "Excuse me? Tex has been with us for well over a decade. He even took over as foreman after his daddy took the fall for Senior a few years back."

"And?"

"And I think you're underestimating his loyalty."

"Am I? Did you already forget that it was a cowboy who took that money from the Russians and let them into *your* warehouse?"

Cross frowned. "And it was Tex at the bar the night you were taken and tortured. He knew where you were. Told me as much the next morning."

River's soft gasp drew all of our attention. "Tex is the one who brought me that package. The one with the pictures."

The way Cross and Walker both snapped their focus to her had me tensing, readying myself for a fight.

"What the fuck are you talking about? What pictures?" Cross snarled.

River's fiery stare showed no hint of fear. "The ones I've been getting since before I came back. Pictures of my parents. Photos that prove they were murdered because of their ties to Twisted Cross Ranch."

"And you didn't think to mention those to me?" he asked.

"I didn't know who was sending them. For all I knew, it could have been you."

"Oh, that's cold, ladybug."

Cross ignored his brother, instead shooting River a hurt-filled look. "But you told Bishop?"

She shrugged, not so much as apologizing as explaining as gently as she could. "I'd just found out he was a fed. I was reasonably sure they weren't coming from him and figured he could help me figure out who was sending them."

"And when you realized it wasn't me?"

"So sorry for not keeping you in the loop, husband. I sort of got kidnapped before we ever got a chance to talk about it. And I mean, if you want to get technical, you *did* find out when I did. I only just pieced together that Tex—and through him Volkov—were the ones behind it."

I wasn't going to push the issue that she had kept the letters from him, regardless if she knew who was sending them or not. She did what she thought she had to, and she'd come to me for help. That was enough for me.

Cross moved until he was standing beside her, his hand slipping around and squeezing her nape. "No more secrets, sparrow."

"Deal. The next time I get creepy unsigned packages in the mail, you'll be the first—"

I coughed, and her eyes lifted to mine before she sighed and rolled them.

"First*ish* to know. I will make sure one of the three of you knows as soon as I do."

"Better," I murmured.

When it was all laid out like this, it was pretty hard to ignore. Tex's hands were all over this. He'd been there at every turn, playing a vital role in Volkov's games, all while hiding in plain sight.

"I'm willing to bet he's the one who let the kidnappers onto the property too," I said softly, hand reaching for a weapon I wasn't wearing.

"Motherfucker," Cross swore.

"He's the reason Bear is dead." River's voice was a low accusation.

"Tex *is* a goddamn mole," Walker breathed, his hands fisting on his thighs, his expression murderous. "I'm gonna kill him."

"Not if I get there first," I promised.

"No. He's fucking mine," Cross argued. "And I'm gonna make it slow and painful. You fuck with my family, you don't live to repeat the experience."

A shadow fell over the patio as Ransom appeared in the wide open space left by the telescoping patio doors. "Uh, sorry to break whatever this is up, but it looks like y'all have company coming."

I stiffened. "No, we fucking don't."

"Sensor was tripped a few seconds ago. I'd say they're about fifteen minutes out. Two black SUVs. No plates. Windows blacked out."

"Tex?" Walker asked.

I nodded. "Seems likely. He probably ran a trace while you two were on the phone."

"Which means he brought Volkov with him," Cross said.

Surprisingly, it was River who seemed the most calm about this sudden turn of events. "Well, we'll just have to throw him a little welcome party, won't we? Ransom, where do you keep your guns?"

twenty

. . .

River

"I don't know why you're asking where his guns are. You're not getting anywhere near that fucker, sparrow. Ransom, where's your panic room?"

I stood, shrugging out of Walker's attempted hold on my arm. "You are not locking me up like I'm a child, Cross. I have as much of a bone to pick with that Russian asshat as you do. More, even."

"Doesn't mean I'm going to let you throw yourself in the line of fire." The insufferable cowboy stepped toward me, trying to intimidate me with his presence.

"Good thing I'm not asking for permission."

This bossy fucking man I was married to was going to drive me to drink.

Cross looked to Bishop for backup, but my giant's silvery gaze was locked on me. "You know how to use a gun, siren?"

"My daddy taught me when I was ten. Bear made sure I kept up with my target practice." A little pulse of grief went through me at the memory. I had my own issues with Dominik Volkov, but it was for Bear that I really needed to do this. He never would have died if he hadn't come here for me. Because I asked him to.

"Get her a gun," Bishop said, turning his attention to Ransom.

Cross's teeth ground together hard enough that a muscle in his jaw popped, but he nodded.

Surprisingly, it was Walker who protested, getting to his feet with a growl in his words. "You can't be fucking serious. We just got her back from them. Ladybug, please let us handle this. Your safety is so much more important than a vendetta. I can't . . ." His voice cracked, and he had to clear his throat before he could continue. "I can't lose you again. I won't."

I rested my palm on his arm, my heart tugging at the emotion in his voice. "Which is why you'll be right there beside me. I understand why you want to lock me away and keep me safe, but I have to do this, Walk. For Bear. I'm a fighter. I have been for a long time."

My gaze flicked to Cross before I could stop myself. The ghost of our past was there in his eyes. He knew exactly why I'd become a fighter. I went to him, curling my arms around his waist and tucking my head into his chest so he knew it wasn't an accusation. Just the truth. If not for him, I wouldn't have left home. I wouldn't have had to learn how to stand on my own. If anything, I was thankful for the lesson. It saved my life.

Cross pulled me closer, dropping his head and brushing his lips across my forehead. "I love you, sweetness. I just want you safe."

"That's what we all want," Walker agreed.

"Then let's kill the asshole and make sure he never hurts anyone again," I snarled.

"That's my girl," Sterling said.

Pride bloomed in my chest as I turned my attention to Ransom, a silent demand on my face.

"Follow me. I have just the thing."

TEN MINUTES LATER, we were back in the main living room, the telescoping glass doors closed once more.

"Why does this house have so many goddamn windows?" Bishop grumbled.

"So sorry my vacation house is more resort than fortress. I'll try to do better with the next one."

I rolled my eyes at the pretentiousness of the statement.

"You had a damn arsenal downstairs. It's a bit of a fortress," Walker said. "Even if you didn't have a rocket launcher."

Ransom laughed. "Guess you'll have to make do with the shotgun."

Walker patted the butt of the firearm strapped across his back. "Me and Rosie are just fine."

"I can't believe you named your gun," Cross muttered.

"My gun," Ransom corrected. "I want her back."

Sterling and I rolled our eyes. He'd gone with the sniper rifle and a second Glock, planning on heading to the roof as soon as the cars came into view. I'd selected one of Brett's revolvers for myself since it was what I was most familiar with.

The air was thick with nervous energy as we waited, watching with bated breath for the Russians. With each moment that passed, restlessness got the better of me.

"Where are they?" I asked no one in particular.

Ransom surprised me with an answer. "Looks like they're waiting. The cars are stalled at the end of the service road."

"Anyone get out of the cars yet?" Bishop asked, all of us turning to face Ransom, who was staring at the security feed on his cell.

"Hard to say. I didn't know how many were in the cars to begin with. They were already parked before I'd pulled up the feed on my phone, and who knows if they let anyone out en route."

"So we know fuck all," Cross said. "Excellent."

"We know they're here. That's better than the alternative," Bishop said.

None of us needed a reminder of what happened the last time they'd caught us off guard. If any of my men got hurt because of me, because of Volkov's sick obsession with owning me, I would never forgive myself.

"Fuck," Ransom breathed.

"What is it?" Walker asked.

"He's alone." Ransom showed us the screen, and sure enough,

there stood Dominik Volkov in a pristine black suit, looking for all the world like he was just here for a business meeting.

The head of the Bratva lit a cigarette and leaned against the side of the SUV as he smoked.

"Where's Tex?" Walker asked.

"Hopefully he's digging his own damn grave," Cross answered.

Without warning, glass exploded inward as shot after shot broke the silence of the afternoon.

"Fuck! Everyone get down," Bishop shouted, pausing only long enough to point at Cross, but my husband already had me on the floor, his big body shielding mine. "Cover her. She gets so much as a scratch, you're answering for it."

I barely had a chance to catch him before he raced from the room, but terror had me shouting his name. I couldn't let him go without some kind of acknowledgment. "Sterling!"

While Cross and I took cover behind a heavy leather couch, Bishop glanced over his shoulder at me.

"Come back to me."

He winked and left without another word. I couldn't help but notice he hadn't made me any promises.

"Bishop's trained most of his life for shit like this. He'll be fine, darlin'," Walker said from his position beside us while the spray of bullets continued.

"They're in the fucking trees," Ransom growled.

"How'd you miss that?" Cross demand.

"I think they fucked with the cameras somehow."

"It doesn't matter," I said before they could keep bickering. "Bishop will take care of them."

"Until they figure out where he is," Ransom shouted, popping up from where he was hiding behind the loveseat and firing off three rounds into the brush.

"Not helpful," Walker said as he popped up to do the same.

I made to push up and help, but Cross kept me down with a hand on my back while he took aim and fired off several rounds himself.

"Let me help!" I demanded.

"Not until they stop shooting. I'm not risking you with a stray bullet, sparrow."

Silence fell in the trees for the briefest moment.

"What's happening?" I whispered.

"They're not gone. They're reloading," Ransom explained. "Stay down."

The sharp crack of a rifle shot echoed. Once. Twice. A third time. Someone shouted in Russian, and I knew Bishop had taken some of them down.

Pride flowed through me, along with the need to participate. I wasn't here to play damsel; I was here to avenge Bear's senseless murder. Not giving Cross a chance to stop me, I jumped to my feet and whipped out my gun, taking aim at the figure I saw moving toward the house. I held my position just like my father taught me. Everything went quiet and still around me as my focus centered solely on my target. I breathed in, my finger squeezing the trigger as I exhaled.

I was a little rusty, but my bullet only strayed a little from where I was aiming, hitting the Russian in the chest. He faltered, but managed to get one shot of his own off.

"River!" Cross shouted, shoving me aside as he moved into the space I'd just occupied. I tumbled sideways as I went down, my eyes never leaving him as my mouth opened on a silent scream.

The bullet tore into his shoulder, blood spraying from his back as the slug went clean through and embedded into the wall.

"Cross! Fuck."

He grunted in pain but didn't stop, taking aim with his other hand and firing until he was out of bullets. Blood soaked his shirt rapidly, running down the light gray fabric, the stain spreading too fast.

"Cross, get down!" Walker shouted just as something came flying into the room, landing with a deafening boom and a blinding flash.

We fell back together, Cross on top of me, my ears ringing so loud it was all I could focus on. Muffled shouts came from above me, and Cross's frantic eyes found mine as he took my face in his hands. His lips moved, but the words didn't register. I couldn't get my bearings. Nothing made sense until, finally, the world came into sharp relief again.

"Get her out of here, Walk."

"No, I'm not leaving you," I said, fear digging its claws deep. His pallid complexion proved he'd already lost far too much blood. What would happen if I left him now? What if I never saw him again?

"Yes, you fucking are. This isn't a game, River. These men are here to kill you, or worse, take you."

It said a lot about the kind of man Volkov was that being taken was the worse of the two options.

"Cross," I whimpered.

His grip on my face tightened briefly before his lips crashed into mine. "You are the most important person in my world, baby. I can't lose you. Not when there's still a chance for you to get free. Go. Please."

Ransom army crawled over to us, reaching into his pocket and fishing out a set of keys. "Take the yacht. Get to the other side of the lake. A car's already waiting."

"How'd you manage that?" Walker asked, taking the keys from him.

"I always have an escape plan. Or three."

The cryptic response must have been good enough, because Walker took my wrist in a rough grip, pulling me away from his brother. "Come on, ladybug. We got to go."

I knew this was the smart play, but my heart protested every step. "Ransom, help him."

He gave me a solemn nod. "You have my word."

It was going to have to be enough. With only a second left, my eyes clung to Cross's, drinking in every detail possible. Memorizing what they could.

"I love you," he mouthed.

"Go! I'll cover you," Ransom urged.

"I love you too!" I shouted as Walker started to run, my arm still in his unyielding grip.

Barely processing my surroundings, I followed Walker as gunfire punctuated our flight. It was a war zone, and we'd become refugees.

"This way," Walker said, his voice tight as he dragged me down the dock. "We have to trust they'll get out of this."

I nodded, clinging to the hope that Bishop would take care of the remaining men so Ransom could get Cross the medical attention he needed before it was too late.

"Hurry, River, Dom's still out there. Ransom lost sight of him when they started shooting. He could be anywhere."

God. Would this nightmare never end?

Another bone-rattling bang echoed from the house, and I couldn't help myself; I looked back and saw smoke pouring from the broken windows.

"Walker," I wailed. "They're not going to get out."

"You can't worry about them right now."

"How can you say that? Your brother is in there!"

"And I promised him I would take care of you. You are the only thing that matters, River."

"Not to me."

"We outnumber you, three to one. Deal with it."

I would have laughed if my heart wasn't breaking into a thousand pieces.

He walked up the gangway, then as soon as he stepped onto the boat, turned and held out a hand. "Trust me. Trust *them*. This is what Bishop does. They'll get out of this."

The reminder that Sterling had survived far worse situations went a long way toward easing my anxiety. He was an ex-SEAL; he could kill men with his bare hands. He wouldn't stop fighting until the bitter end. I couldn't think of a better person on this planet to watch my husband's back.

I looked around the thirty-five-foot ship, wondering why the hell Ransom had a yacht on a lake before the answer came to me. Because he could. It was his private lake. What other reason mattered when you had more money more money than you knew what to do with? I was willing to bet this wasn't his only boat. He probably had a whole damn fleet.

"Get below deck. I'll take care of the ropes and launch us as soon as I can."

"I can help."

"No. River, I know your independent streak is strong, but I need you to listen to me this once, please. Get below."

Walker rarely spoke to me with such a commanding tone, but I could tell he meant it. With a sharp nod, I made my way downstairs and into the cabin. It would have been nice to experience this level of luxury if we weren't running for our lives.

There were a couple of bumps which I imagined was the rope hitting the deck as Walker worked to unmoor us. Sooner than I expected, I heard footsteps coming down the stairs.

"All done?" I asked, turning around to greet him.

But it wasn't Walker staring back at me with a malicious grin. "Hey there, Mrs. Cross."

Dread was an icy fist around my heart as I stared at Tex. The man had a gun pointed at me and nothing but hatred in his eyes.

"Proud of yourself, you fucking traitor?" I spat.

He let out a bitter laugh. "I'll be even prouder after I watch the life leave your eyes."

I shook my head, struggling to figure out why this man hated me so much. "What did I ever do to you?"

"Personally? Nothing. But those motherfuckers are obsessed with you, and I can't wait to see the expressions on their faces when they realize I took away the only thing they cared about, just like they did to me."

I wasn't familiar with the history between Tex and the Crosses. "Who did they take from you?"

It was like watching a dam burst. Rage twisted his face as the words poured from him. "My family. My father gave Senior everything, and what did he get for a lifetime of loyalty? A bullet to the brain and an unmarked grave. You have any idea what that did to my mama? Not knowing why her husband was hauled off to jail for a crime he didn't commit? Why he never came home after his supposed escape? Those bastards ruined my family's name. Robbed us of our honor. And they couldn't even do her the courtesy of telling her the truth. Instead she drank herself to death."

My stomach churned. "Senior was a heartless bastard. But Cross and Walker . . . you're like fami—"

"Shut your goddamn mouth. I'm nothing to them. Just another disposable goon. But not anymore. Now they're the ones who will be disposed of. Maybe I'll send them pictures of your corpse first. Draw it out and make them suffer like I did."

He seemed taken with the idea, his focus turning inward as he played out the scenario in his mind. Seeing that he was distracted, I slowly reached behind me for the gun holstered in the waistband of my pants, only to come up empty. My gun wasn't where it was supposed to be. Fear stabbed deep into my chest. I must've lost track in the confusion of our escape. *Stupid, River.*

"Now, be a good girl and cry for me, Mrs. Cross. Put on a good show for your snake of a husband." He held up his phone as he approached, pressing his gun up against my forehead.

I backed away, shaking and frantically scanning the space for something I could use as a weapon but coming up empty. My shoulders hit the wall, and terror finally won as tears spilled down my cheeks. I wouldn't make it out of this. Not if I didn't fight like hell.

Bringing my knee up as hard and fast as I could, I made contact with his balls, knowing he might pull the trigger but fully aware I was dead anyway. Thankfully he'd underestimated me, and instead of squeezing off a shot, he doubled over.

I didn't waste a second, making a break for it, screaming Walker's name and racing toward the stairs, only to be pulled up short by a fist in my hair.

"Not so fast, you stupid bitch."

Stars exploded behind my eyes as he threw me to the floor, the back of my skull hitting the floor a second before his fist collided with my cheekbone. Tex stood over me, gun trained on my head.

"I wish I could say it's been a pleasure working for you, but—"

Tex's words cut off as his entire face exploded outward, blood and bits of brain spraying all over me before his body slumped forward. I rolled away just in time to avoid being crushed by him.

"River! Fuck, are you hurt?" Walker was there, hands on my wrists, gently pulling me to him.

"I'm okay. It's not my blood," I said with a tremor in my voice as a flashback to the last time I'd been covered in another man's gore flickered through my mind. "God, Walker, he was going to kill me."

"Not on my watch. I'm sorry it took me so long to get down here. Fucker clocked me in the back of the head." He wrapped me in a fierce hug, his racing heart pounding beneath my ear.

"You got here just in time."

"Thank fuck for that. I'd never forgive myself if I'd been too late."

I stopped him with a kiss. "It's not worth thinking about because you did. I'm alive. I'm safe. Because of you."

"We'd better get the fuck out of here."

"What about the body?" I said, through chattering teeth as shock set in.

"That's Ransom's problem. I just want to get you out of here."

We climbed the stairs to the upper deck on shaking legs, each of us leaning heavily on the other. Me because my limbs were trembling with the aftereffects of adrenaline. Walker, because he'd pushed himself too hard on his still healing leg. I could see it in the lines of his face, drawn tight with pain.

Walker and I had only just made it to the upper deck when we once again stopped short.

"Fuck."

I didn't need him to elaborate. There was no missing the flashing lights or sirens wailing in the distance. The cavalry had arrived, but not before one final gunshot rang out.

twenty-one

• • •

Cross

"You good?" Ransom asked as the gunfire finally stopped. "I think they're dead."

One could hope.

"I'm not fucking good. But I'm alive."

For now. My fingers were icy, and I didn't think that boded well for me. Breaths labored, I leaned against the back of the sofa as I pulled myself up to my feet. Only sheer force of will kept me upright as the room spun. Blood dripped to the floor, soaking my jeans and making a puddle at my feet. Shit, I couldn't afford to lose any more. All I could hope for was that Walker'd gotten River out safely. That was all that mattered.

"I'm calling it in, Cross. Get your story straight. There's no way we can clean this up." Ransom pulled out his phone.

Fuck.

The last thing we needed was a bunch of police crawling around, but Ransom was right. There were too many bodies. We'd have to rely on the almighty dollar to keep our asses out of the interrogation room this time. Thank God the fucker was loaded. He put my fortune to shame.

I stumbled as I tried to stand without anything holding me up, but I managed to get myself under control. I would walk out of this fucking house on my own.

"Here," Ransom said, tossing me a blanket. "Put pressure on your shoulder."

"It's not gonna help. Too late for that."

"Don't be a fucking asshole."

"Volkov's still out there," I reminded him. "He's just waiting us out."

Ransom's mouth opened to respond, but the sound of slow clapping and the crunch of glass interrupted whatever he was about to say.

I twisted around, biting back a groan as pain lanced through my wound.

"So nice of you to wait for me," Dominik said in his thick accent, lips curling in a smug smile.

The bastard thought he'd already won.

"You're late, you fucking coward," I said through gritted teeth.

"You say late. I say right on time."

"Your men are dead."

He shrugged. "They knew what they were signing up for. By the way, I have to thank you for providing me such a lovely locale to claim my prize."

"You talk too fucking much," Ransom said, pulling his gun and taking aim. He pulled the trigger, but nothing happened besides an impotent click.

Volkov laughed, pulling out his own weapon. "Mine is fully loaded, I assure you. Should we try that again? Once more, with feeling?" He aimed the gun straight at me.

Ransom was a blur as he rushed the Mafia don. Dominik didn't even blink. He twisted, bringing the butt of his weapon down on Ransom's temple and sending him crashing to the floor, unconscious.

"Alone at last," he mused.

With each sluggish beat of my heart, more vital blood left my body. But I refused to die without taking this motherfucker with me.

"The way it should be," I said, raising my pistol and proud of myself when my arm remained steady as I chambered a round.

Volkov surprised me by laughing. "It's like the old cowboy movies, no? Pistols at high noon? Where's your hat, Cross?"

"Must've left it at home."

"Pity. But perhaps they'll find it in time to bury you with it."

"Do you practice your villain lines?" Fuck, my voice was a harsh rasp, but I couldn't let him have the parting shot.

His grin turned cutting. "No need."

Fucking prick.

"Ransom was right. You talk too fucking much."

He kept his gun on me but gave a little shrug. "Excuse me for enjoying my big moment. I must admit I've been looking forward to it."

"Dying?"

He made a soft tsking sound. "No, I'm not the one dying here today, Cross. I meant taking her right out from under you. Again."

"The fuck you are. You're never touching her again." I squeezed the trigger and fired.

Volkov laughed, a slightly shocked sound, like he couldn't believe I fucking missed.

Frankly, I couldn't either, but I was woozy as fuck and seeing double. So I probably hit the mirage version of him, at the very least.

"Pathetic, just like your father said you were when I killed him."

"He died of a heart attack."

"I know. Poison is a wonderful tool. Not just a woman's weapon. You should have seen his face when he realized what I put in his drink."

Before my mind could begin chasing the dozen questions that brought up, I sneered and chambered another round. "Good thing I'm nothing like my father."

"No? The apple doesn't fall far from the tree, as they say."

He could have killed me more than once by now. The asshole was toying with me. Letting me bleed out instead because he knew I was done for.

In the distance, I caught sight of Bishop as he dropped from the balcony with the lithe grace of a cat. He stood, drawing his service weapon, and held one finger to his lips as he approached Volkov.

The best thing I could do now was let Bishop sneak up and take the shot, meaning I needed to keep the asshole talking. Good thing he seemed to be a chatty fuck.

"Thanks for doing the job for me. No one much liked my dad, anyway."

"I'm going to enjoy dismantling your family's empire piece by piece and getting richer while I do it. But I think my favorite part will be filling your widow up every fucking night."

I saw red, but before I could do anything, Bishop pressed the muzzle of his gun against the back of Dominik's skull. "Don't move, motherfucker."

The Russian went still, the smile melting away as if it had never been there at all. He fired without warning, and I dove to the floor in a display of desperation rather than skill. The bullet missed by the grace of God, embedding itself into the wall behind me.

"What the fuck are you doing? Take your damn shot," I shouted at Bishop when the sound of a scuffle reached my ears. I pushed up on shaking limbs, finding Bishop wrenching the gun from Volkov's hand before twisting both arms behind his back.

"Dominik Volkov, you're under arrest."

"No!" I shouted. "What the hell are you doing? Kill him!"

Enraged, I got to my feet, struggling for every second as I staggered with purpose toward where Volkov was bound and on his knees. The gun trembled in my hold, but still, I pressed it to the fucker's forehead and readied myself to end him.

"I'm not gonna miss this time, asshole," I rasped, each word a fight.

"Cross," Bishop said with an urgency I hadn't heard from him before, "if we take him in, more people than just you will get justice. Think of all those girls. All those families. They deserve to know what he did. To know he's going to get the death penalty. If he dies here, his secrets die with him. None of those victims will get closure."

Indecision, the fucking bastard, wormed its way through me. My resolve faltered. I'd killed men with barely a second thought for doing less than Volkov had done.

"River . . ." I whispered, pleading with him.

"I know. Listen, I'll look the other way. If you want to kill him, I'll help you bury the body. But justice is sweet when it's served."

Tears blurred my eyes, and a sound of pure rage burst from my throat as I lowered my gun. "You better make damn sure he gets the chair, or I swear to God I will hunt him down and slit his throat, consequences be damned."

"You have my word, Cross. He'll never see the light of day again."

Locking eyes with Bishop, I nodded. "Make the fucking call."

Bishop gave me a sharp nod, pulling a few zip ties out of his pocket.

"Where the fuck did those come from?"

"I grabbed them when we got the guns. Better safe than sorry," he said, getting to work restraining Volkov.

The bastard chose the wrong damn moment to laugh. "You are such a pussy. No wonder your wife was so easy to take from you. You don't have the balls to do what needs to be done."

I brought my arm back and hit him with all the strength I had, the pistol connecting with his temple and sending him slumping over unconscious. "Shut. The. Fuck. Up." Every word was a chore.

I had minutes at best before I ended up right there beside him. Falling to my knees, I dropped the gun. My limbs were numb, eyes so heavy I could barely keep them open.

"Fuck, Cross. Hang on," Bishop said. I heard him make a call, but there wasn't anything left for me to stay awake for. "Can you call someone?"

Ransom's groggy voice reached my ears. "Shit. Yeah. Hang on." He continued talking, but it was clear he was on the phone. "Bring the chopper. He's hurt bad. And call Garrett, have him on standby at the hospital. No one treats one of my guys but him."

I had the fleeting thought that if Walker was still here, he would have made a 'get to the chopper' joke. God, I hoped he got her out. I hoped I lived to see her again so I could make sure she knew she was safe and loved. That she didn't need to worry about Volkov touching her ever again.

"Cross, stay with me. Come on, man," Bishop said, real fear in his voice.

"Tell River I'm sorry." I slurred. "I always loved her. Always."

I heard the sirens just before I lost the battle with consciousness and faded into the darkness.

twenty-two

. . .

River

Two weeks later

"It's okay to cry, River. You loved him. If you can't cry after his funeral, when can you?" Gigi said, her voice thick with tears as she passed me a tissue.

"I just can't believe he's gone. It happened so fast, and I didn't even get to say goodbye. I loved him so much, you know? I woke up this morning and expected him to walk through the door, and then I remembered he was gone, and it was like seeing his dead body all over again."

My lower lip trembled as the tears I'd been battling all day finally spilled down my cheeks. The funeral was over, but the hurt remained. I didn't think it would ever lessen. The hole he left in my heart would never heal.

A warm palm splayed across my lower back. Instant comfort washed over me as the familiar scent of my husband's cologne followed.

"Come here, sparrow. It's been a tough day." Turning around, I stared up at the face of one of the men I'd love for the rest of my life. Behind him stood Walker, Bishop, McCreedy, and Ransom, all wearing somber expressions.

They'd orchestrated this funeral for Gigi and me, knowing we needed to give Bear a proper sendoff. Private and secret though it may have been. As far as the government was concerned, he was a missing person. But we knew the truth. That was enough for us.

Cross pulled me into his chest, holding me close. It took everything in me not to break down into soul-wrenching sobs. I'd done more crying in the last two weeks than I had in my whole life.

As a figure dressed all in black came into view, I had the sinking suspicion my tear-filled days might not be behind me just yet. Wilson, Bishop's handler, finally graced us with his presence.

"What the fuck does he want?" Walker asked, the question posed to Bishop.

"Fuck if I know."

McCreedy let out a heavy sigh. "He's probably here to arrest the lot of us."

"What?" Gigi asked, eyes wide. "But I didn't do anything."

"Calm down, hellcat. I doubt he's here for you." Then he pulled out his phone. "But just in case, I'll get a head start on bail money."

Bishop dropped a kiss to my forehead, giving my nape a squeeze before he started toward his boss.

"Sterling," Cross called, stopping him in his tracks. "You let him come to us. We face this together."

It did something to me, that show of camaraderie. Daniel Cross Jr. didn't stick his neck out for many, but I guess when someone saves your life, loyalty is second nature. Bishop had donated his blood to Cross that day at the hospital. If it hadn't been for him, this funeral would've been for my husband, not the brother of my soul.

I threaded my fingers with Cross's and gave them a reassuring squeeze. He didn't know how much this meant to me, to see them all become a unit, a family. And not just for my benefit, but because they'd survived what was essentially a war together and genuinely cared about one another.

Cross leaned down, lips brushing my ear as he whispered, "Go to him. He needs you."

Slipping out of his hold, I reached for Sterling and offered him a sweet smile as he met me halfway, his touch a gift I knew he didn't give freely.

"It's okay," I said, my gaze not leaving his silver one. "Whatever happens, I love you."

"I love you too."

He only had a chance to give me a brief kiss before Agent Wilson was upon us.

Instead of approaching Bishop, he turned to me, holding out his hand, his eyes hidden behind mirrored sunglasses.

"Mrs. Cross, I'm sorry we have to meet under such somber circumstances."

I raised a brow, not taking his proffered hand. "Am I supposed to know who you are?"

Technically, I knew he was Sterling's FBI superior, but only because we'd discussed it once. Agent Wilson didn't know that, though, so as far as he was concerned, he was still a complete enigma to me.

"Deputy Assistant Director Wilson, ma'am. Forgive the interruption, but I'm here on official business."

Here it was. The moment he took us away. Bishop for deserting his duty, me for killing my kidnapper, Walker for the death of Tex, and Cross for . . . fuck, everything. I was going to lose it all.

He pulled an envelope out of his jacket, offering it to me.

"What's this?"

"Those are the official documents declaring you as Sterling Bishop's sole beneficiary."

I blinked. "Excuse me?"

"Agent Bishop was a remarkable man."

"Was?"

I cut a glance to Bishop, who was standing beside me, his expression inscrutable.

"Yes. Isn't this his funeral? I know you two weren't legally married, but he did name you as his partner and beneficiary in his living will."

He sighed heavily and refused to make eye contact with Bishop. "It was the hardest thing I've ever done."

"What was?"

"The paperwork regarding his death in the line of duty. He died a hero, Mrs. Cross. The man will be a legend at the Bureau. Volkov was a boil on the ass of humanity."

Walker spit out a laugh, "That your official take, Agent Wilson?"

Wilson grinned. "Let's just say I eagerly await his day in court. As do the families of well over a hundred victims."

"Jesus," Walker breathed.

"And what about us?" Cross asked.

"What about you, Mr. Cross? As far as I can tell, you're spotless. Not a single blemish on your record. Almost as though it was wiped clean. Your father's sins died with him."

Walker coughed before bringing a flask to his lips. "Shit."

Ransom gave Walker a droll glance. "Is the flask really necessary? You have an entire bar right fucking there. Would you like me to make you a drink?"

Walker took another long drag out of his flask. "Why would I dirty a glass? This is Langston whiskey in a flask monogrammed with the ranch's logo. I'm good."

Ransom huffed out a breath and shook his head. "Langston. Those Montana assholes sure know how to make some spirits, as much as I hate them."

I would have laughed if I wasn't so worried this was all some kind of massive joke.

"Mr. Wilson—"

"Doug, please."

Walker snickered. "Doug. Your best friend named Skeeter, by any chance?"

I had no idea what he was talking about, and it was clear by the expression on Wilson's face this was not the first time he'd heard that joke. "Is he finished?"

"No," Walker said. "I'm a font of entertainment."

I caught his eye and shook my head. *So not the time, Walker.*

"So Sterling is *dead,* and I'm his beneficiary?"

Wilson nodded. "Exactly."

"And Cross and Walker are exonerated?"

"Seems that way."

"And after today, I never need to worry about you showing up unannounced again?"

"Precisely."

Sterling shifted next to me but didn't say a word. He knew better than to question such a gift. I supposed I should take a page out of his handbook and do the same. But after what we'd been through, I couldn't help but feel like the other shoe was going to drop. Eventually. I hated that I felt this way about my life, but it had been one thing after another, and I was convinced nothing good lasted forever.

"Best of luck to you, Mrs. Cross. Take care of yourself." He handed me a thick business card. "If you need anything, feel free to reach out."

"What about Volkov?" Cross asked, his voice a harsh rasp.

"I'm not at liberty to say."

"That's bullshit. If anybody should get to know—"

Wilson cut off Walker's protest with a well-aimed glare. "I'd say you've received all the favors you deserve, wouldn't you? Don't press your luck, Mr. Cross."

Walker shuddered. "Mr. Cross is my grumpy ass brother, thank you very much."

"I am not grumpy."

"Well, not if you're getting laid."

My cheeks burned at the truth in Walker's words. "Thank you for coming, Agent Wilson. Drive safe. We've got it handled here. I'll call if I need anything."

Wilson gave us one last nod and turned back to leave the way he'd come. Gigi let out a soft whistle. "Is it just me, or did he give off some real big dick energy?"

McCreedy glared at her. "No. Not even a little. If you ask me, he was all hat and no cattle."

She snorted. "I didn't ask you, jackhole. I was talking to River."

His glare intensified, and suddenly I was picking up vibes of my own. Jesus, these two could start a wildfire with the sparks they were throwing off.

As soon as Wilson's car was out of sight, I turned to Sterling. "Did you know?"

"Did I know what?"

I slapped him gently on the shoulder, instantly regretting the uninitiated contact, but he didn't even flinch. "You know exactly what. I'm your beneficiary?"

"You are."

"Since when?"

"Since the gala."

I gasped. "What? Why?"

"Because the moment Volkov made me, I knew it was only a matter of time before my ticket was up. I needed to ensure you'd be taken care of, no matter what happened to me or the Cross brothers."

"Sterling . . ."

He shrugged, entirely unfazed. At least if you didn't know how to read the hunger burning in his quicksilver gaze. "I didn't know you were the one my heart was searching for, but the second I found you, there wasn't a doubt in my mind. Your name is etched on my bones, siren. Whether you were mine to keep or not, I was always yours."

Tears pricked my eyes. Sweet mother of God, would these men ever stop taking me out at the knees?

"I didn't realize the giant had it in him. I'm gonna need to up my game. I think he just out-swooned me." Walker's whisper broke through my tears, turning them into a watery chuckle.

"That's why I don't even try. I just use my dick." Cross's frank admission had me laughing as Sterling pulled me in for a kiss.

"I'm sorry, have you forgotten what I'm packing? Magic fucking cross, brother. Magic fucking cross."

"Fuck off. I don't need trinkets to get the job done. Just pure fucking skill."

"Okay, cowboy. Let's see which one of us she screams for first, shall we?"

"We are right fucking here. Jesus," Ransom said.

Gigi socked him in the arm. "Shut up. Don't ruin this for me. I am living vicariously. Although to be honest, I'm tired just thinking about satisfying three men. That's a lot of dicking, and I need my beauty sleep."

"I'm sure you could take it," Ransom teased.

She batted her long lashes at him. "Are you offering to help me test the theory, handsome? I've never had a cowboy of my own before."

McCreedy cleared his throat. "Not under my fucking roof. Come on, hellcat. Funeral's over. I've got work to do."

Gigi sighed and rolled her eyes. "Work, work, work. That's all he ever does. I can't wait until I get my own place and can start over properly."

"What?" McCreedy and I said at the same time.

"Yeah, well, if you guys would stop eye-fucking each other for two minutes, I'd finally be able to tell you. I'm staying here. I don't have anything waiting for me back in Hemlock Harbor. Bear is gone. You're here. So it makes the most sense for me to put down roots where the only family I've ever known is. That's you, River Adams."

Cross cleared his throat.

I rolled my eyes. "Technically I never changed my name."

"Easily remedied."

"Someone is feeling mighty big for his britches." I might've pushed back, but I secretly loved his domineering, jealous side.

Cross just held my stare, his gaze knowing. I hated that I was the one who folded first, but fuck, the man made me hot with nothing more than a look. He always had. And he knew it too. "I'll make an appointment for your name change this week."

Pursing my lips, I fought a grin. He didn't know I already asked McCreedy to file the paperwork. I wanted to be a Cross, but even more than that, I wanted to incorporate all my men. Since I couldn't legally marry all of them, I had to get a little creative, but once the paperwork went through, I'd be River Sterling Cross. My former FBI agent didn't love his last name because of the trauma it carried, but he did love it when I called him by his given name. Renaming myself, giving up my middle name in favor of his, was a way to keep them all with me. And, as far as the public was concerned, I would still be Mrs. Cross. I couldn't wait to hand them all copies of the judicial decree once I got it. I could already imagine the night we'd have in store for us.

Fuck, I was wet just thinking about it.

A night with all four of us together at the same time wasn't something we'd done yet. We'd toyed with the idea but never taken it that far. That didn't change the fact that it was one of my greatest fantasies.

Gigi elbowed me with a soft cackle. "I recognize that blush, woman. You're thinking about getting laid."

I sputtered. "Am not."

"Pfft. Bear would be horrified, but I'm proud of you. Get it, girl. Do you know how many books I've read where she gets herself a whole stable of hotties? God, this is like one of my favorite series, except you're not the harbinger of the apocalypse . . . right?"

"Uh . . . not to my knowledge."

Gigi looked at Cross, her eyes narrowed with mock suspicion. "You didn't use to be a priest, did you?"

"Uh . . . no?"

"Secretly Irish?"

"Definitely not."

"Bummer." She turned to Sterling. "Any chance you enjoy howling at the moon or long naked runs through the forest in your wolf form?"

"What?"

"Never mind. How 'bout you, Walker? Any Norse blood in those veins? You know"—she did a cheeky little jig—"Thor in the streets, Loki in the sheets?"

Walker just laughed and shook his head. "I'm too sober for this conversation."

"Speaking of sober, I think it's time to go home. You're definitely plastered," McCreedy said, taking her arm.

She rolled her eyes at Jackson before slapping his hand away and looking back to me. "I'm glad one of us is getting laid. Don't get knocked up, though. I hear it comes with consequences." Then she waggled her brows. "You know what? Fuck it. Get knocked up. Your baby might end up saving the world."

Cross joined Bishop and me, a low chuckle rumbling from deep in his chest as he leaned in and pressed a kiss to my shoulder. "Maybe she's on to something, sparrow."

"You think?"

"I did promise to put my baby in you once the danger had passed. I feel like this counts."

"Not if I get there first." Sterling gripped my waist a little tighter.

"'Scuse me, assholes. Did you forget that I've got dibs?" Walker spluttered.

Gigi opened her mouth, but McCreedy covered it with his palm before she could pipe up.

"You love scrooge!" she shouted behind his palm as he took her to the car.

I think I only understood her because of our years together. McCreedy didn't seem to catch the muffled insult. He'd have hell to pay when they got back to his house.

"You know I wasn't kidding, ladybug. I did call dibs on the baby making. Cross got to marry you and be your first. It's only fair I get to give you a baby before him."

"It's not really something you can control, Walk," I said with a laugh, my cheeks flaming, but not with embarrassment. The promise of what they were offering was more than welcome. I wanted everything with them. A family. A future. A life filled with love and laughter.

And lots and lots of orgasms.

A happy shiver worked its way through me, settling between my legs. How had I gone from so sad to so horny in a matter of minutes?

Looking from Bishop to Walker, then finally to Cross, I realized it was one hundred percent because of them. The three men who were made to love me. Forever.

Sterling pressed a hot, open-mouthed kiss to my neck. "What are you thinking about, siren?"

"Forever."

"Seems like a mighty long time," Cross said.

"Or not long enough." This came from Walker, a smile spreading his lips.

I shrugged. "I guess it depends on how you look at it."

A smile brightened Cross's face. "I suppose you might be right."

"You all heard that, yeah? Did someone make a note of the time? I think the world just ended after all. Daniel Cross Jr. just said I was right."

He growled. "Don't make me regret it."

"Oh, I plan to let you prove me right over and over."

"About what?" he asked, looking at me with surprise.

"That you belong with me. All three of you. I said it years ago. We were destined to be together. It just took us a decade and an FBI sting to make it happen."

"Technically it was a missio—" Bishop started, but Walker silenced him with a slicing motion across his neck. "Never mind."

"Whatever the reason, I'm thankful fate threw us together. It may not have been a pretty road that got us here, but that doesn't mean we can't enjoy a happy ending."

"I'll show you a happy ending."

"Jesus, Walker. It's a wonder you ever get your dick wet. You're a fucking child."

"Magic cross, brother. Magic cross."

"Can confirm. It's magic." I laughed, love shining through every word.

This was the life I'd been waiting for. The one filled with happiness I'd been promised in every fairy tale my mama told me. Except instead of one prince, I had three, and we rescued each other. But one thing remained constant. We'd found our very own version of a happily ever after.

The end . . . for now.

epilogue

. . .

Walker

One week later

I adjusted my hat as I approached the gazebo where River had instructed me to meet her tonight. I didn't know why I was nervous, but the note she'd left me had been so vague I couldn't help but feel something was up. My only question was whether this was a good surprise or a bad one. We'd had our fill of bad ones to last a lifetime.

The curtains surrounding the gazebo—those were new—rustled, and excitement got the better of me as I eagerly waited for my woman to show her face. Instead Cross's ugly mug greeted me, and my shoulders slumped in disappointment.

"What took you so fucking long? You're late," he grumbled.

"According to this here note, I'm right on time."

Cross's eyes narrowed when he discovered me instead of River. "What the hell are you doing here?"

"I was summoned. Just like you, it'd seem."

"That explains the bedding."

My eyebrows shot up with interest. "What bedding?"

He gestured behind him. "The gazebo's all done up like some sort of sultan's paradise. Blankets, pillows, snacks, fairy lights, the whole shebang."

"I didn't forget an anniversary or something, did I?" Worry gnawed at my belly. "Oh fuck, am I already failing at the boyfriend thing?"

Footsteps on the gravel behind me had my heart lurching, desperate to see River so I could atone for forgetting whatever it was I'd missed. Once again, I was disappointed.

"Dammit, Bishop. You are much less curvy and soft than the woman I want to see right now."

His scowl matched mine. "I could say the same about you two. Any idea what this is all about?"

Cross shook his head while I shrugged. "Your guess is as good as mine."

He scratched the back of his neck before pulling a folded manilla envelope from his back pocket. "I bet it has something to do with this, but it says not to open it for another two minutes."

"And you're really gonna wait until the exact time?"

He turned the envelope around so we could see River's bold scrawl.

DO NOT OPEN EARLY. (THAT GOES DOUBLE FOR YOU, WALKER).

DON'T TEST ME UNLESS YOU WANT TO GO CELIBATE FOR THE REST OF YOUR LIFE.

"Damn, ladybug. Way to call me out."

"We're supposed to meet her inside the gazebo. Not stand around here like a bunch of rodeo clowns waiting for a bull," Cross said, jerking his chin toward the curtained-off enclosure.

"Fine by me. I love a good snack." I waited for Bishop to follow after my brother, then did the same, walking into a romantic as fuck setting.

Cross hadn't been lying. If the crimson curtains hadn't been extravagant enough, the hanging lanterns and string lights took care of that, casting everything in a romantic glow that made me think of that one musical I'd sat through for River when we were teens. Tufted velvet pillows in rich jewel tones littered the space, along with silk and faux fur blankets.

"Damn, y'all. I think our girl's intent on a seduction tonight. Perhaps this is less about surprise and more about living out her fantasies."

Cross's low growl wasn't one of disapproval or jealousy. We'd been holding back with her since returning from Ransom's. It was important to us all that River heal before she jumped into anything so intense. But not a one of us would tell her that. No way in hell. If she knew we were being careful, she'd be madder than a hornet. She'd made that clear enough the night she called me out, but on this point, the three of us were agreed. No need to rush into anything when we had the rest of our lives to spoil her rotten.

Bishop held up a giant ostrich feather. "What do you think this is for?"

"If you need me to spell it out for you, you're not invited to the party."

He bared his teeth at me in a snarl. "Just try to kick me out. I dare you."

Before he could make good on the threat, his phone went off.

"You set an alarm?" Cross asked.

He shrugged. "I don't mind following the rules. Especially when she's been so good about following mine."

"Fair point."

"Well," I demanded, my impatience rising. "Are you going to open it or what?"

"Careful, little Cross, or I won't tell you what's inside."

"Oh, fuck off. It's a magic cross, and I promise it's not remotely little."

Bishop pulled open the envelope and tugged the paper out, his eyes immediately going wide, then a little glassy.

"Jesus, what the fuck is it?" I glanced from Bishop to my brother. "I think I hate this guy."

"She . . . shit . . . She changed her name to Sterling."

"WHAT?" Cross shouted. "No, she fucking did not."

"Yeah, what he said," I added.

Bishop shrugged. "See for yourself." He ignored my outstretched hand and passed the paperwork to my brother. Motherfucker.

I waited for Cross to drop the hammer, but a smug smirk twisted his lips instead. "River Sterling Cross. That's my fucking girl."

My heart swelled beneath my ribs, making it hard to breathe. "She actually did it? She took our name?"

Part of me expected Cross to emphasize that it was *his* name, but he didn't. For once, he let me entertain the possibility that she was as much mine as she was his.

"I wanted to carry all of you with me."

The three of us spun toward the opening where River stood, looking like a fucking goddess. Her long hair was down and curled around her shoulders. Her dress was white, but not in a bridal way. It was a collection of sheer panels and lace. It reminded me of a grown-up version of her birthday dress, back before I thought I'd lost her forever.

Bishop whistled while Cross let out a reverent, "Wow." I, however, was struck fucking dumb. My tongue felt too big for my mouth. And was that drool? I swiped at my chin. It was definitely drool.

Be cool, Walker. Jesus.

Might as well just jizz in my damn Wranglers while I was at it.

"You're as pretty as a picture, darlin'," I finally said when I remembered how to talk.

Her cheeks flushed the sweetest pink as she approached me, threading our fingers and staring at me like I was the only one in her world. It might not be the case, but it sure as hell felt like it right now.

"We might not be married, Walker, but I have your name. I'm a Cross now. Forever."

A sharp jab in my side had me throwing Cross a murderous glare. Did he really have to ruin this for me?

But the look my brother was giving me brought me up short. It was one that pleaded for me to pay attention. I followed the intentional dip of his head and saw our mama's ring glittering from the center of his outstretched palm. Fuck, was he letting *me* have this moment?

Brow furrowed, I almost didn't take the offering, but he cleared his throat once, and I took the band of precious metal before sinking down to one knee right there.

"What are you doing?" she asked.

"Only seems fitting that a woman we both love wears our mama's ring."

Tears misted her eyes, and her hands immediately lifted to her lips. "Were you two carrying this around the whole time?"

Cross shrugged. "It was Walk's idea. I was just waiting for the right time."

"Don't sell yourself short," I said, knowing he needed to be as much a part of this moment as I was.

River held out her left hand, her fingers shaking. "Well, what are you waiting for?"

"Not a damn thing, beautiful," I murmured, sliding the ring onto her fourth finger.

Bishop came to stand behind her, gazing over her shoulder at the ring she'd hopefully wear until the day she died. "It's perfect."

"Just like the woman wearing it," Cross agreed.

"Oh my God, stop being so swoony. It was supposed to be my big moment, you jerks."

"I can't help it if it was always you, sweetness. Even when it shouldn't have been, it was you." Cross's voice broke a little there at the end, and I understood him on a deeper level than he realized.

"I feel the same. I spent my life loving you quietly, but now? Prepare yourself for me to love you so loud the whole world knows it, ladybug."

"I like loud," she said with a smile.

"I know." I waggled my brows as I got to my feet and pulled her in for a kiss. Then, turning my attention to Bishop, I asked, "Does it bother you the ring doesn't incorporate you? We can figure something out."

The stoic man shook his head. "She's got my name. That's all that matters."

"I do have another finger, you know. In case you ever want to get me something of your own," she teased.

"I didn't take you for a jewelry girl," Bishop said, raising a brow.

"Oh, I don't know. I think there's a time and place for everything. Maybe you should check that envelope one more time," she said mysteriously, her lips twitching with barely suppressed glee.

Cross was the first to catch her meaning. His eyes narrowed suspiciously. "What did you do?"

She played at zipping her lips while Bishop emptied the remaining contents of the envelope in his hand. Three platinum bands slid into his calloused palm, each with a little ribbon bearing a name.

"We're on the same wavelength, it would seem." Her voice was quiet but filled with resolve. "I never want to be apart from any of you, and if I'm carrying your names with me, you should have part of me too."

She took Cross's ring and untied the ribbon before sliding it onto his finger, then Bishop's, and finally mine. Inscribed inside mine was *W & R*. My fucking heart swelled all over again.

"I love you, darlin'."

She smiled. "I love you too. All of you."

One by one, we took our turns kissing her stupid. By the time Cross released her, she was flushed and starry-eyed. Seemed like the perfect time to make my move.

"Do I get to test out these feathers on you now?" I asked, tickling the side of her neck with one of the oversized plumes. "It's basically our wedding night, you know?"

Her wicked grin did something to me. Something I really fucking liked.

"Yes. You absolutely do."

Not one to be outdone, Bishop let out a low chuckle. "First one to make her scream gets to take her ass."

"You're on," Cross said before I could.

We may not have taken her as a team before, but something told me we were going to be experts at it before the night was through.

Bishop

"ON YOUR KNEES, SIREN." I may have sounded confident, but if I was being honest, she'd shaken me to my core. No one had ever wanted me enough to do something like what she'd done.

I didn't need vows or a big ceremony. This was enough. It was fucking everything.

All that was left to do now was blow her mind so she never had a reason to regret her decision to tie herself to us forever.

And it would be forever. She was mine now. Ours, I guess.

I would never let her go. I'd follow her from this life to the next.

Or if I went first, I'd haunt her and be there to welcome her to the other side.

Like I said, for-fucking-ever.

She blinked at me, her eyes wide as my words sank in.

"You're not wasting any time, are you?" she asked, sinking to her knees.

"No. I've wasted too much already. I want your mouth on me, eyes rolled up to watch mine as I feed you my dick."

"Jesus. Is that hot? I think that might be hot," Walker whispered, confusion leaching through his tone.

Cross grunted, but I knew he wasn't immune to the image either. Last time he watched me fuck River's face, he had front row seats and begged to join in.

"She can take turns sucking off each of us if you want to learn first-hand just how hot it is," I offered. Look at me being magnanimous. Truth was, I had a pretty good idea what the suggestion would do for our girl. If I reached down between her thighs, I knew I'd find her dripping.

"Yes."

That was all it took. One ragged whispered word. Walker and Cross both made quick work of their clothes, stripping down to nothing as I slowly unbuttoned my shirt.

"Should I get naked?"

"Is the pope Catholic? Fuck yes, ladybug."

She giggled, pulling her dress up and over her head and revealing her lush body in all its naked glory. "Just checking." Her gaze flicked down to Walker's straining erection, and pure hunger flashed in those eyes when she looked back up at me. "You're still dressed."

"I'm working on it. I do like knowing you're desperate for me, though."

"You can't blame me for being eager. I've dreamed about having all three of you for months, and it's finally happening."

Cross reached down, dragging his thumb over her lip before pushing the tip in and waiting expectantly. "Suck it, sweetness." She did, her wide eyes on him the whole time, waiting for his praise. "No one is blaming you for anything, sparrow. You're such a good girl." She hummed around his digit before he pulled it free with a loud pop. "You know what to do, baby. Mouth on his cock, just like he taught you. Show Walker and me what you learned."

There was a part of me that wished it wasn't Cross in the driver's seat right now. Technically I'd been the one to direct her to her knees, after all. But something about the way she obeyed him had my dick jerking in my Wranglers. I really needed to get out of these clothes, but she was damn distracting.

"You ready for me?" I asked, my voice a deep rasp.

"Always."

My lips hitched up. "That's my girl."

I held her gaze while I pulled my zipper down, my cock thick and heavy, a bead of precum smeared across the tip. Goddamn, the way she licked her lips as she stared at me made my balls pull tight, threatening to send me headlong into an orgasm I wasn't prepared for.

The last thing I was going to do tonight was blow my load before I was good and ready.

And no, it wasn't just because I was competitive.

At least not entirely.

Letting out a soft moan, River leaned forward and wrapped those perfect lips around me. My hand shot out of its own volition, fingers tightening in the hair at her crown as I fought to keep from rocking my hips forward so I could fuck her throat.

"Christ, you're beautiful," Walker breathed.

"Thank you," I said, unable to help myself.

Walker gave me a look that said what I could do with my gratitude, but any comeback I had was lost to the eye-rolling pleasure of River's tongue swirling across my frenulum.

"Fuck, baby. Just like that." My fingers gripped her harder. "You're such a good fucking girl, remembering everything I taught you."

On either side of me, the Cross brothers took themselves in their own hands. Walker utilized long, slow glides while his brother opted to squeeze himself hard at the base. River took all of this in with a rapt expression. The hunger in her eyes was unmistakable.

She pulled off my cock and stared up at me, lips swollen, a line of saliva trailing from the head of my dick to her bottom lip. I knew what she wanted. To take turns with us.

"Go on, siren. Make them feel good like you did for me."

I realized my mistake a second too late. I'd given her permission, but not a complete order, meaning she now had to choose which brother to pleasure first. Indecision warred in her gaze; she didn't want to disappoint either of them.

Walker saved the day by making the decision for her. "Dibs, darlin'. Get those pretty lips over here and wrap 'em around my dick."

I watched her take him, tongue circling the ball at the end of each of his piercings, wondering to myself how the fuck I was in this situation. I'd never wanted to watch my girl with another man's dick in her mouth, but this? This was fucking sexy. She gave herself over to all of us in a way I couldn't have fantasized about in my wildest dreams.

Cross was just as impatient as Walker. After River took Walker all the way to the root a few times, the elder brother reached for her. "My turn, baby."

Walker let out a strangled protest, but didn't take the fight any farther as she backed away and smiled up at him.

"Don't worry, cowboy. I'll be back. I promise."

I stroked myself slowly, very aware of how tight my balls were and just how close I was to coming all over my own hand.

Apparently I wasn't the only one, because it was only a few bobs of River's head over Cross before he shot me a look I had no trouble interpreting. He'd go off like a rocket if she kept it up much longer.

I gave him a single nod, letting him know I understood.

Without a word, he took River's hair in his fist, pulled her off his dick, and turned her face toward mine. "Suck," he growled, making her whimper.

If he thought I stood any chance of making it through this, he was dead wrong. That fact was proven the instant she swallowed my length.

"Fuck, River. Your mouth is so good. Keep it up, baby. Take it all the way."

She let out a garbled moan, and Walker cursed in response, fist flying over himself.

"Maybe we should come all over her? We can shower her off and come back?"

I liked the idea more than I'd expected to, a warning tingle building at the base of my spine. "Fuuuck."

I wasn't the only one into the idea. River's hand snaked between her legs, giving me the opening I needed.

"Not so fast, siren. You're not in charge of your pleasure. We are. Hands off."

She did as I said, but she was squirming with need, her thighs squeezing together as she chased some kind of friction to ease the building ache.

"On your back, spread those legs wide for me."

"Oh God," she moaned as she pulled free of me.

"Walker, hold down her arms. Cross, get her ankles."

"Where will you be?" Walker asked.

I caught River's eyes and purposefully licked my lower lip. "I'm on cleanup duty."

"Cheater," Cross grumbled.

"No. I'm just smarter than you are."

Before long, I was face down, drowning in her perfect fucking pussy. The sounds I made were near feral as I devoured her, loving the way her thighs quivered around my ears.

"God, Sterling. I'm so close. Fuck. Fuck."

She writhed against her Cross brother restraints, so I pressed one palm on her lower belly, pinning her in place before my other hand went for her cunt.

"Oh my God. Oh my God."

"Scream for me, siren. Come all over my face."

"Fuck," Walker grunted, hips thrusting in the air almost without conscious thought. "I'm not gonna fucking last."

"You're not even inside me yet, Walker."

"I know. God, I fucking know."

Cross made a sound low in his throat. "Make her fucking come or get out of the damn way so I can."

"Come for me. Right. Fucking. Now." I slid a second finger inside her and stretched my pinkie back so it pressed against the rim of her ass.

That was all it took.

River devolved into a series of incoherent screams, bucking wildly against my face while my tongue lapped at her clit and my fingers continued their sensual assault on her body. I didn't stop what I was doing until her thighs clamped onto my head.

"Too much. Too much."

Pushing back onto my knees, I winked at her as I wiped my chin on my forearm. Then I looked up at Walker. "I win."

"I beg to fucking differ," Cross said.

"Yeah, man, that was a group effort."

"It was my face she was riding. You want the credit, you gotta do the work."

"With pleasure." Cross released her ankles as I got to my feet, the two of us doing a carefully choreographed dance to avoid touching.

He stood over River, staring down at her with a look of pure heart-breaking love. I understood him better than I ever anticipated was possible.

"It should be the lady's choice. Where do you want me, sparrow?"

Cross

RIVER'S heated stare pinned me to the spot as she bit her lower lip and got to her knees. "Are you really giving me the reins, Danny?"

A fire lit inside me at the nickname. She was riling me up on purpose, messing with the bull because she not only wanted the horns, she craved them. We were an electric current in a summer storm. Wild. Unpredictable. Dangerous. But in all the best ways.

The two of us would never be boring. We had too much fight in us for that.

"Call me that again and see what it gets you, wife."

A soft giggle escaped her. "How are you going to stop me, *Danny*?"

I growled, giving her all of two seconds before I grabbed her by the nape and pulled her in for a desperate kiss. I didn't care that she'd just sucked off two other men. All I wanted was her lips on mine.

"I'll make you choke on my dick," I growled against her mouth.

"I thought it was my choice."

"You telling me you want something else?"

"No. That's exactly what I want. You in my mouth, pumping me full of your cum. Walker underneath me, those piercings of his lighting me up inside, while Sterling takes my ass."

"Jesus," Walker said, drawing the name out as he went. "Anything you say, darlin'."

Bishop seemed content to let us lead, staying a bit back while we got in position.

"You got any lube, siren?"

She nodded and pointed to a small basket off to the side.

"Good girl," he murmured, pressing a kiss to the top of her head as he went to grab it.

"Open wide, baby," I said, rubbing the weeping tip of my dick across her lips. "I'm not gonna last long this time."

"Fuck, neither am I," Walker admitted. "You're so wet. I'm sliding all over."

"Try to hold on for me. I want us to all come together this first time," she begged.

"You better hurry, then," he said.

She opened her mouth, and I didn't need another invitation. I pressed forward, filling her with my thickness as she sank down on Walker. I knew only because he barked out a harsh curse, and she whimpered around my cock.

"Hold her for me. I need to stretch her a bit."

Bishop's gravelly command was the only reason I knew he was back. I was too focused on the play of River's tongue along the bottom of my shaft to notice what the others were doing. I preferred it that way, to be honest. No matter who else was with us, this would always come down to me and her.

"Fuck that's nice," I grunted, threading my fingers through her hair and holding her still so I could set my own pace. If I left it up to her, I'd be blowing in a matter of seconds. "You suck my cock so good, baby."

River stopped, her whole body tensing as something changed. My gaze went to Bishop, who'd lined up behind her and was focused as hell as he slid his dick inside her ass. The way she writhed made me determined I'd get her there next time. Especially if it meant I could pull sounds like the ones she was making out of her.

"Fuck, she's not gonna last. She's gripping me like a damn vise."

"Me too," Walker panted. "God, it's a tight fit with you stretching her like that."

My hips jerked erratically as she swallowed around me, her moans causing little vibrations to climb up my shaft. I was gonna come. I couldn't hold it back anymore.

"Play with her clit, Walker. I need her to come." My words were a strained plea as I fought off the waves of pleasure bearing down on me.

Walker must have done as I asked because the sounds River made grew frantic.

"Just let us do the work, baby," Bishop said, his voice laced with pleasure-filled tension. "All you have to do is take it."

"Goddamn, she's coming around my cock." Walker groaned, clearly finding his release.

When Bishop tensed behind her and cried out her name, I realized I was the last man standing. For about point-five seconds. I spurted down her throat with a groan that could have been a plea or a curse. Maybe it was a bit of both. Either way, my climax had me seeing fucking stars.

A bit of my cum escaped the corner of her mouth as I pulled out, the pearly drop trailing down her chin before I caught it on my thumb. "Waste not, want not, sparrow." I pushed my thumb into her mouth. "From now on, I'm coming in you. Every. Single. Time."

"Speaking of next time," Bishop said, pressing a kiss to her temple while his fingers ghosted across River's neck, "how about you make him come with your mouth while my hand is wrapped around your throat?"

"Oh God," she whispered.

"You give me five minutes, we can test it out here and now," Walker said.

"Promise?"

"Always."

"There's no rush. We have all night."

"I think you mean the rest of our lives, Mrs. Cross," I said, fully aware of the emotion bleeding through in my voice.

She yawned despite her best efforts to hide it, and I guided her down onto the nest of blankets and pillows waiting for us before I snuggled in behind her. She was the perfect little spoon to my big one as her round ass tucked into my pelvis.

"You know," Walker drawled, coming to join us, "they say spooning leads to fucking."

"I think you mean forking," River said sleepily.

"I said what I said."

Bishop slid into place on the other side of her before Walker could. "That's what I'm counting on."

"They also say sharing is caring, asshole," he sulked, taking a seat by River's head and pulling one of the blankets onto his lap.

"You put a lot of stock into whoever *they* are."

Running my knuckles back and forth over River's shoulder, I listened to my brother and Bishop pick at each other with a smile on my face. I finally had what I'd convinced myself was never possible. The woman I'd sworn to love and protect from the shadows.

It may not have played out exactly as I'd planned, but I couldn't complain. I spent nearly a decade thinking it would never happen, period. I'd take whatever I could fucking get. And if I had to share her, I couldn't think of two better men to help me give her the life she deserved.

She was ours. Forever. And nothing was going to change that.

"I love you, Mrs. Cross."

When she didn't answer, I leaned up on my elbow and saw that she'd already drifted off, a blissed-out smile playing across her lips.

"Well, would you look at that. I think we wore her out already."

Bishop shook his head. "No way. She's just recharging for the next round."

"I call dibs on her ass," Walker said.

I chuckled. "Dibs never seems to work out for you."

"The law of probability—"

Bishop shoved Walker away, making him break off with a laugh. "Get out of here with that shit before you put us all to sleep." Despite the gruff words, he was smiling when he met my gaze.

"This how you imagined it?" I asked him.

"Imagined what?"

"Retirement."

A low chuckle rumbled from his chest. "Not in my wildest fucking dreams. I thought I'd go out in a blaze of glory, but I wouldn't change a damn thing. This way, I get to die doing the thing I love."

"River?" Walker piped up.

Bishop laughed. "Yeah, I suppose so."

"I get it, man. We feel the same way. She's our world. Always will be. And now, we get to ride off in the sunset, knowing she'll be ours for the rest of our lives."

"When you put it that way, seems like one of those fairy tale endings," Walker mused.

"And they all lived happily ever after," River murmured.

I grinned. "They sure fucking do."

Curious about whether Bishop got to show River what he can do with a rope?

Visit themategames.com/TCRbonus to download a Twisted Cross Ranch bonus scene.

Or if you prefer to listen, you can download the audio version at themategames.com/TCRbonusaudio.

acknowledgments

To our Alpha & Beta readers: Kat, Tara, Suzi, Catherine, Hannah, Megan you're early feedback and enthusiasm is the wind beneath our wings (or words, we guess…or should it be hooves because #cowboys?)

Jason, JF, Aaron (and our best bitch Stella) You can't spell cowboy without J, J, A…never mind. But seriously, we couldn't think of three more well suited voices for these guys. Thanks for helping Stella make another sandwich (they're sort of her favorite).

Tyler & Ashley we're so glad you haven't gotten off the ride yet. Please never quit us.

Mo, what would we do without you giving our boys the spitshine they deserve? And for teaching us how to spell. And when to capitalize. You're the sexiest first grade teacher of all time.

Tiffany, thank you for making our covers beautiful and bringing our vision to life.

Wander and Andrey, we love you both and never thought we'd have a daddy like you, Wander. We're already counting down the days until our next Vegas pool party.

KP thanks for holding our hands when we needed it, and being there to keep our strategy straight.

Gabe thanks for keeping us both fed and watered when Kim comes to visit. Especially for the Pornstar martinis (and ogre serenades) and taking care of us when we got deck sunburns. You didn't sign up for two wives, but you got them anyway.

Wade, Betty, Henry, Luke, you're the best emotional supporters we know.

Lastly, thanks to Tim McGraw for making Kim cry. You can expect her therapy bill in the mail.

more by meg & kim

the mate games universe

By K. Loraine & Meg Anne

War

Obsession

Rejection

Possession

Temptation

Pestilence

Promised to the Night (Prequel Novella)

Deal with the Demon

Claimed by the Shifters

Captive of the Night

Lost to the Moon

Death

Haunting Beauty

Hunted Beast

Hateful Prince

Heartless Villain

also by meg anne

Brotherhood of the Guardians/Novasgard Vikings

Undercover Magic *(Nord & Lina)*

A Sexy & Suspenseful Fated Mates PNR

Hint of Danger

Face of Danger

World of Danger

Promise of Danger

Call of Danger

Bound by Danger (Quinn & Finley)

The Chosen Universe

The Chosen

A Fated Mates High Fantasy Romance

Mother Of Shadows

Reign Of Ash

Crown Of Embers

Queen Of Light

The Chosen Boxset #1

The Chosen Boxset #2

The Keepers

A Guardian/Ward High Fantasy Romance

The Dreamer (A Keeper's Prequel)

The Keepers Legacy

The Keepers Retribution

The Keepers Vow

The Keepers Boxset

The Forsaken

A Rejected Mates/Enemies-To-Lovers Romantasy

Prisoner of Steel & Shadow

Queen of Whispers & Mist

Court of Death & Dreams

Prince of Sea & Stars

A Standalone MMF Romantasy Adventure

Gypsy's Curse

A Psychic/Detective Star-Crossed Lovers UF Romance

Visions Of Death

Visions Of Vengeance

Visions Of Triumph

The Gypsy's Curse: The Complete Collection

also by k. loraine

The Blackthorne Vampires

THE BLOOD TRILOGY

(Cashel & Olivia)

Blood Captive

Blood Traitor

Blood Heir

BLACKTHORNE BLOODLINES

(Lucas & Briar)

Midnight Prince

Midnight Hunger

THE WATCHER SERIES

Waking the Watcher

Denying the Watcher

Releasing the Watcher

THE SIREN COVEN

Eternal Desire (Shifter reluctant mates)

Cursed Heart (Hate to Lovers)

Broken Sword (MMF menage Arthurian)

STANDALONES

Cursed (MFM Sleeping Beauty Retelling)

REVERSE HAREM STANDALONES

Their Vampire Princess (A Reverse Harem Romance)

All the Queen's Men (A Fae Reverse Harem Romance)

about meg anne

USA Today and international bestselling paranormal and fantasy romance author Meg Anne has always had stories running on a loop in her head. They started off as daydreams about how the evil queen (aka Mom) had her slaving away doing chores, and more recently shifted into creating backgrounds about the people stuck beside her during rush hour. The stories have always been there; they were just waiting for her to tell them.

Like any true SoCal native, Meg enjoys staying inside curled up with a good book and her fur babies . . . or maybe that's just her. You can convince Meg to buy just about anything if it's covered in glitter or rhinestones, or make her laugh by sharing your favorite bad joke. She also accepts bribes in the form of baked goods and Mexican food.

Meg is best known for her leading men #MenbyMeg, her inevitable cliffhangers, and making her readers laugh out loud, all of which started with the bestselling Chosen series.

about k. loraine

USA Today Bestselling author Kim Loraine writes steamy contemporary and sexy paranormal romance. **You'll find her paranormal romances written under the name K. Loraine and her contemporaries as Kim Loraine.** Don't worry, you'll get the same level of swoon-worthy heroes, sassy heroines, and an eventual HEA.

When not writing, she's busy herding cats (raising kids), trying to keep her house sort of clean, and dreaming up ways for fictional couples to meet.

www.ingramcontent.com/pod-product-compliance
Lightning Source LLC
Chambersburg PA
CBHW020501310726
48979CB00016B/2753/J
* 9 7 8 1 9 6 1 7 4 2 1 1 6 *